A Fabrication of Gold

John Moat

Laura, I would say
you were minted SM
material — one I hope
this handbook will give
you one or two ideas
for besic household
maintenance.
Much Love,
John.

the @rite factor

First published by The Write Factor 2011
www.thewritefactor.co.uk

ISBN 978-0-9568735-0-7

Copyright © John Moat 2011
www.johnmoat.co.uk

A CIP catalogue record for this book
is available from the British Library.

Cover design by Simon Willby
Printed in the UK on recycled paper by ImprintDigital.net

ALSO BY JOHN MOAT

POETRY
Thunder of Grass
6d per annum
The Ballad of the Leat
Skeleton Key
The Welcombe Overtures
Fiesta & The Fox Reviews His Prophesy
Firewater & The Miraculous Mandarin
Practice
The Valley
100 Poems
Hermes & Magdalen

NOVELS
Heorot
Bartonwood
Mai's Wedding
The Tugen & The Toot
Blanche

SHORT STORIES
Rain

ALSO
The Founding of Arvon
A Standard of Verse
The Best of Didymus

AND WITH JOHN FAIRFAX
The Way to Write

In Memory of Barbara Bapty

NB: To counter false expectation relating to trades description,
it should be made clear that SM in this book is Soror Mystica,
or Mysterious Sister. Good to have got that straight.

SM is giving her instructions – her voice that brown husky colour, deadpan. The same slow weight whether she's scolding the muscovy or pronouncing her eternal moony verities.

I open my eyes and catch her looking down at me – momentarily it's a glare, a tigerish amber, before she can draw down the customary shade of alternative green.

She's saying: "You need to write it down. You're good at writing, aren't you? Okay, so just write it down like it's a dream. That way it's the dream writing itself. Only you're awake."

I think: I am awake am I? I'd rather hoped I was dreaming. And anyway what does she know about writing? I mean about me never getting round to it.

I'm lying on her kitchen floor. On a mattress. If this isn't a bad dream then the dream must be... must be about every other part of my life.

SM sniffs and wipes her nose on her billowing sleeve.

I think: See, business-like. She's not as willowy as she and the advertisement would have me think.

But she hasn't finished – I can't be sure she'll ever be finished.

'"Being awake's what's important. Not high or dreaming or out of your mind. And you do need to write it down..."

"Write what down?" *There, I've managed to get a word in, though it sounded strangled, more of a squeak.*

"All of it. Writing's a way of being awake and staying with your dream or whatever you've been into. By staying with it, it's able to really be there, it's able to begin to work. That way you can begin to change..."

Her voice washes on with something of the brown monotony of floodwater. But since the sniff I'm pretty sure there's steel somewhere at the back of it – in the same way as behind the billows of ethnic calico there's this business-like smell of sweat.

I glance up at her. I'm thinking: Young lady, if an inability to change were my problem I wouldn't be here. You don't go selling up everything if you can't countenance change. Everything that is except the one thing that's going to safeguard my seat at the Rotary, in other words, the little 'conservatory' side of Fiona's late father's Garden Centre. Which was to be the doddle I could run from home – which indeed is how at one point it did seem to have turned out (good Japanese products, adaptable to the customers' individual needs and tastes, easily assembled by a small team of skilled locals). Ability to change – how else would we in our mid-forties, early mid-forties, have achieved what we'd never fully planned: idyllic early retirement, a move to the deep country, the chance to develop our own garden, and finally the chance to write... To write what? You name it. Thrillers? Well perhaps not thrillers. Since the appearance of Mr Caruso I think I'll be giving thrillers a wide berth.

I say suddenly: "You mean I should write down everything, or just this... this, this sort of what do you call it, this 'inner business'?"

SM looks down at me from her high stool. One eyebrow raised. I think she's picked up the panic in my voice. Well I am, I'm in a panic. Not at all like the me I recognize, but I am. Not only are conservatories not a doddle, but suddenly they're out of fashion and the bottom's fallen out of the market. I've invested an arm and a leg... two legs, at least one of which is Fiona's. They could be the finish of me. They could be the finish of everything. No more Rotary lunches. And Annabel... no more college. She'll have to get a job as a... as a... I suppose it could even come to that. But that's not my real problem, which is how on earth do I come to be here lying flat on my back? Actually I know the answer, it's because... it's because I've completely lost my head, most of my wits and... all my marbles.

SM says: "One day you'll need to go into that."

"I beg your pardon?" She will talk as if she's R.D. Laing or someone.

"Your voice – you mean like you didn't notice?"

What have I said? I didn't think I'd been saying anything. But before I can say anything I hear myself say: "Oh that, that was the man in the mirror."

So there, it's out, I mean in the open.

She says: "Well done. So we meet the man in the mirror. You see, when things are really happening the inner business is the outer business. So now you're into it, and now you just write whatever wants to write itself."

Another sniff, more of a snivel. This time it's me.

"But where do I begin?"

She smiles at that.

Always it's something else she seems to be smiling at. It's not easy to tell where she's smiling because her expression has never changed. Green eyes, unhung-up lips that look like they've just mouthed the word 'moon' – even her thick fox-brown hair held at the back with a kind of leather buckle and wooden skewer – they all have that attentive spaced-out look.

"Begin with the first thing that wants to get itself written. Why not with India? That would be the beginning. Right?"

How come she knows I was born in India?

There, I only have to wonder and she's tapping the side of her nose. She lets her eyes widen like opening the green interior of a wood and whispers, "A quick moment, passing through, a whiff of cardamom, with a hint of patchouli... oh, and a little after-taste of gripe water."

"Gripe water!" At least that was what I was going to say when, from somewhere, almost certainly from way down inside me, a distraught little voice starts calling, "Ayah!"

1
WALKABOUT

1

No doubt about the first thing that wants to get itself written. Caruso.

We're out of orders. I would say the business was definitely on the rocks. An inexplicable slump in the demand for conservatories.

I'm in the kitchen thinking this through. First to go will be the photocopier. Then the answerphone. Then Jennie. No, Jennie first.

Fiona's doing the ironing. Methodically. A neat pile. This is where I break the news.

"No," I say "this time it's worse. Far worse."

Fiona's looking at me, the lines (two vertical, one horizontal) pronounced between her brows and in her eyes the meticulous grey outweighing the blue to show there's something she doesn't understand. "But love, the conservatories aren't everything. If it goes go bust it's not the end of the world."

What I say next startles me: "It may not be the end of your world." I wouldn't normally expect to say that. But what I'm thinking is: She's thinking she takes after her father, it was her father's business, she could run this business with her eyes shut. Well she's not running it, I am – and if it were to fail I would... well, that would be the end of it. The end of everything. In fact it would be *the* end. Finale. Finish. Full stop. Over and out.

Fiona's still looking at me – there are now two horizontal lines. I can see that whatever's on her mind its not the fall in the market.

"Never mind, I'm sure you'll think of something, love."

I want to say: We're not going to think our way out of trouble this time. The climate's changed. The entire world's becoming a greenhouse. People in the know are moving out of conservatories into polytunnels and... and hydroponics... and growbags... In this climate Richard Branson wouldn't make a go of it. Our life is about to crash. I'll have to go and work for someone. And Annabel, no more college, she'll have to go out to work. But I say nothing, because whenever Fiona looks at me like this I never do manage to say anything. It's a trick of hers. She shuts me up by never before having been anything like so beautiful. Twenty-three years she's been able to do this, to shut me up. Something she does with her eyes. The light comes on and it's suddenly all the blue that's predominant. When that happens there's nothing anyone can possibly say.

She goes on: "It's really getting to you, isn't it? Whatever it is, these last two weeks you've not been your usual cheerful self."

Not myself! That's a dreadful thing to say. But then I think, what if she's right... does it mean there's some other man? I say, "Yes, but I'm the one you love. Hey ho."

"Come on, love, don't be silly. It's just you keep getting in a stew."

"In a stew, me!"

"Yes, a right old stew. I'm not the only one who's noticed. Yesterday Jennie was telling me..."

So now I'm in a stew. I see.

"What, you mean, Jennie's been... Jennie!? What would my being in a stew, or a casserole, or a... or a fricking fricassee, what's it got to do with Jennie?"

At which point two things happen at once. First I hear a horrible whinging moan. I look round and realise there's no one it could have come from but me. Unless... it's this 'some other man'. And second, the door of the office flies open and down the five stairs with the kind of inevitability of spilt syrup comes Jennie. She looks as if she's got a temperature. At the same time she has the staring, deep-frozen appearance of someone who's discovered something dead in the bath. And she's done it again – decided to wear that kind of rancid-looking chamois leather miniskirt that makes her thighs appear decidedly unstable.

"Jennie, whatever's the matter?" Not me, that's Fiona.

Jennie's mauve hot fluster is running down into her blue chiffon blouse. It's too much for me. I'm... I'm speechless.

Jennie says: "There's a message on the answerphone. A Mr Careswell. He's interested in a conservatory."

"Caruso!"

"Careswell."

"I dare say. I suppose he's calling from La Scala."

"No, Besseldon Manor."

Fiona is looking startled. She says: "What on earth was that?"

"Was what?"

"That horrible sort of moan?"

Jennie is looking at Fiona as much as to say, "See, what did I tell you?"

I say: "That was nothing. That was me clearing my throat."

"Besseldon Manor," Jennie says dreamily. "He must be ever so rich."

I say: "Jennie, for God's sake blow your nose, what do you mean rich?"

"He says, can you do it in gold leaf? I expect he means those sort of hanging down bits."

I don't say what I was about to say, instead Fiona says, "There, you see, I told you you'd think of something."

2

I've come in from a good stint in the garden. Harvesting the onions: Giant Sturons. I'm in the bathroom washing my hands, and continuing to worry about Caruso.

As it turns out, Besseldon Manor is down a pea-gravel drive. Edwardian stone with kind of brick Tudor chimneys. Outside the front door, a Rolls Royce and a white plumber's van.

I think: Of course, if you're trying to shift good health, you need your drains running on time.

Mr Caruso is planning a health-hydro. Mr Caruso is only about two heads tall, one of which is taken up with an enormous head. In the wings a dark woman twice his size with a dangerous expression. I think: Probably Maria Callas. She's the matron, and it's her that's calling the shots about the conservatory. Mr Caruso's only concern is that they should attract a good class of punter. Hence the gold leaf.

"No problem," I say. "I know just the bloke." That's when I feel the parquet shift. Normally I would never take such a shot in the dark. In any case what is gold leaf? From here on I'm treading deep water.

I say: "You want it all over? Or just the hanging down bits?"

"Just the hanging down bits."

I say: "You do realize this will be an expensive job. I shall be obliged to ask you for a deposit." See? We call it acumen.

Back in the bathroom I've stopped washing. I'm holding the rim of the basin with both hands. Clenched. I've come to this really worrying bit.

Caruso is looking up at me, his hooded eyes pinkish and sleepy, like a vulture who can't eat any more for the moment.

He says: "How'd you like to do yourself a favour, lad?"

It turns out he's a broker.

"Ah, stocks" I say smoothly, "and shares."

The hoods go down slowly over his eyes and then go up again.

"Commodities," he says.

This is the signal for Callas to get busy puffing up the cushions. Caruso leads me into his study. When I come out I've done myself a favour and I've a piece of paper to prove it. At the front door Caruso reaches up and pats me on the back.

"And remember, don't sell us short on the gold leaf, lad" he says.

Back home I explain it all to Fiona in some detail.

Caruso has made me an unrepeatable offer, a chance to acquire a share in a truly priceless commodity.

"You're off your head," Fiona says. "It's drugs."

"No, artefacts. Priceless ones."

"I expect he's robbed a tomb."

"Don't be ridiculous, he's doing me a favour."

The deal is simple. The price of my share is what Caruso owes as a deposit. When the ship comes in the commodities will fetch at least three times that price on the open market. Money for old rope.

Fiona says: "I thought it was artefacts. Anyway where's all this old rope at the moment?"

"It's appreciating," I say. "It's three days out from Penang."

"I think you've lost your Elgin marbles."

"What I think is we're back in business. Big business. Incidentally do you happen to know anyone in the district who does gold leaf?"

I may have sounded confident, but the truth is I'd already begun to worry. Added to which, Fiona was eyeing me in a grey light.

I start washing again, scrubbing my nails. It's then I catch sight of this not very prepossessing character in the mirror. We have an arched pine mantelpiece mirror over the basin. I think: Hullo, how did he sneak in? I'm not sure I like the look of this one.

I think: Someone's set him up to look a shade like me. Except he's sullen as a damp shoe, and the whites of his eyes are all yellowy. Doesn't smell too fresh either, if that whiff's a whiff of him. Smells like a monkey house.

Monkey house... why on earth would I think of a monkey house? India, I suppose. I hear someone say, "Ayah..." Which seems a perfectly reasonable thing to say.

I feel almost sorry for the guy in the mirror – clearly he's lost his zest. Poor devil, his hair's going grey in front of his ears, and he's puffy and pouched under his eyes.

I say: "What's up? Touch of the mid-life ague?" And to cheer him up I try giving him a broad smile.

He bares his teeth. Then his face begins to break up. I think I can hear something cracking. It must be the mirror. I hear him give a horrible groan, which would have been quite enough to scare me even if it weren't somehow being hauled out from between my teeth.

3

There's someone downstairs. Fiona. No, it's Fiona and Annabel. They're at the bottom of the stairs. I can hardly hear what they are saying – but it's clear from their voices it's something they don't want overheard. I tiptoe to the bathroom door.

Annabel's saying: "Oh I see. It's just he's usually so, you know, laid back. Usually he seems pretty much on top of things."

Fiona says: "Don't worry, he's going through a difficult patch. He's in a tizz because he thinks he's made a boo-boo with the business."

For a moment I'm frightened they may have heard me snort. Oh, so it's me who's made the boo-boo. Have they not heard of Mr Caruso by any small chance? It would be nice to be able to rely on one's family for a little support. I bet Callas doesn't hand Caruso this boo-boo stuff.

Annabel says: "Well if that's all it is – thought he didn't seem his usual chippity self. Ta mum, see you this evening." And I hear her run out of the door.

And I hear Fiona start up the stairs.

Two things happen, one hard on the heels of the other. First, I'm trying not to laugh. I'm thinking: Good, back to normal, here's Fiona on her way up the stairs. Second, as she reaches the top of the stairs, fury. My nostrils flare. The air whistles icy-shrill through my teeth. She comes past the open door of the bathroom, carrying towels. Stops with her back to me and opens the linen cupboard.

She's beautiful. She is. She's as beautiful as she ever was. More actually. Even the thread or two of grey in that billowing corn-stubble-brown hair. Long-backed as ever in her blue Shetland jumper, the sleeves up to her elbows. Beautiful. I open my mouth to croon my soft "ooo-whoo!" – my daft love-call these twenty years – and am only just quick enough to slam the trap before the moan can escape.

4

SM says: "Go into it then."

"Into?"

"Yes, the moan. What sort of moan? There are moans and moans. Feel the feeling."

SM – what one might call an ethnic person: long saffron skirt, green blouse, white apron, a kind of Wife of Bath in her twenties. Twenty-six if I had to guess, but could be nearer forty. Could be eighteen. I'm lying on the mattress on her kitchen floor.

I close my eyes. At length I say: "This was a moan that seemed to have been around a long time."

She says: "Usually a problem's been the problem all along. The problem is seeing the problem." All this quietly while she's fishing a wasp from the honey-jar. "When you begin really to see the problem you see it going all the way back."

"You mean," I say to show I'm up with the latest thinking, "back to childhood?"

She looks down at me calmly. "To the hassle of being born usually. Sometimes earlier. Sometimes back to conception. Sometimes quite a lot earlier than that."

Christ!

I think: No, that's somewhere I'm not about to go; to be honest I'm not even keen to be around at my own conception. But I don't want her thinking I'm a sort of flat earth nerd, so I'll tell her something that's not only right up her street but will make her really sit up – I'll tell her about my meditation experience.

Since this Caruso business I've not been sleeping. Which for one reason or another means Fiona's not been sleeping. Fiona's had a consultation with Annabel who as a result of last year's meaningful relationship is now house authority on psychic research, ESP, talking to one's tomatoes, experiential religion, fringe medicine...

Annabel pronounces: "Dad, your not sleeping's probably trying to tell you something."

I say: "That Mr Caruso's done the midnight flit."

"Like, maybe you should start to meditate."

"Meditate? Me? And that would help find someone to do the gold leaf?"

"No, but you might find out about yourself. Then yourself might allow you to go to sleep."

I'm out of my depth so I say: "I see."

I'm about to walk away when I see Fiona's eyes go stormy grey. Quickly I adopt the magnanimity of, was it Naaman the Syrian? – the one who agreed to the daft suggestion he treat his leprosy with a dip in, of all places, the local Jordan. I say: "Okay, lets go. How do I get it off the ground?"

Annabel says: "Of course, I can't let you have my mantra. That's a secret."

"Yes, yes, quite right, of course."

"But I'll give you another. How about *Soahum*? You should be alright with that."

"Thank you. Thanks very much. I expect you'd like a deposit. Or perhaps you can suggest a way I can do myself a favour, lad?"

"Don't be silly, dad. And you can keep it a secret if you want to. All you do is keep intoning it until your mind goes empty."

To which Fiona adds: "You're going to have to do something or you'll just have to lie awake in some other room. I've had being woken night after night to speculate on the progress of your ship from Penang and to share the delights of the dawn chorus."

I say: "Okay, okay. And what's this..."

"Soahum?"

"Yes, what's it all about anyway?"

"Swami said it means, like, what's out there's in here – but dad I don't think there's much point you trying to understand it."

"Swami said..." I say darkly. "I see."

So off I go to the office to give Soahum an airing – not so much the half-lotus as the full-frontal flat on your back position – and zap! I'm asleep on the sofa. Wonderful. I'm into meditation.

A week later something odd happens – which is what I'm eager to tell SM. I'm in my study, doing whatever I do when I think I'm meditating, viz: thinking how I must stop thinking about Caruso. A windy day, the wind making a clatter in the dry winter woods. Suddenly the wind has stopped. I keep my eyes shut and my ears squinting to stick with Soahum – but the entire world has stopped. It's folded its arms, and in steely silence is watching me. A physical sensation, like the moment before one realizes one's in pain. I feel my inside go inky black. What I'd taken for the floor, I mean of the room inside me, isn't the floor, it's a flimsy membrane. And it's beginning to lift. (I'd not intended to treat SM to all this but with the cap once off the fizzer there's no stopping it). I realize I'm having to concentrate to keep this, whatever it is, down. I feel if I were to let go an instant, I'd be a gonner. The force is mixed with the silence. I can feel the bulge of it beyond the membrane, staring and somehow on top of me. I grimace, clench my fists, in the effort to hold it back. Finally I dare open my eyes. I seem to come out of it then, but even so the after-shock of the experience is around for days. I keep feeling the silence, or whatever it is, threatening to come back up. Keep having to stop and clench my fists.

"Off you go, and don't you bother to come back," SM says sternly.

What's this? I'm being fired? Or am I now too hot to handle? But then I see she's actually showing the open window to the wasp. She turns back and looks at me, her face expressionless with clarity.

She says. "Open the window, the wasp flies home."

5

Fiona is still arranging the towels in the linen cupboard. She's singing to herself, half under her breath. She seems very still inside, a warm bubble of stillness. I think: she isn't with it at all, she's wherever she is inside, where I can't reach her. This for some reason makes me determined to... to cry. Then I hear what she's singing.

"Kiss me in the rain..."

I think: It is, it's the other man. Well that's it, so she's going to have to pay for this.

"... makes me feel I'm a child again..." half under her breath, but dreamy and meaning it, like Barbara Streisand.

I think: Twenty years of happiness and she chooses this moment, just when I'm not feeling myself, to have a bit on the side.

I'm feeling perhaps I should hit her or something. Then I have this stupid thought that it's the man in the mirror who's at the back of it. That's the moment she turns and looks at me.

"Goodness," she says, "what's the matter with you? You're not looking yourself."

"And what precisely do you mean by that?" I do, I feel really suspicious. "Maybe you're trying to say I look like this other man?"

I didn't mean to say that, but then I think, why that's pretty clever, I've set a trap. If she says yes, I'll know she's been having an affair. And if she says, now come on love, what on earth are you on about? then I'll know for certain.

"You feeling alright?" she asks.

I think: There you are, she's tricky.

"Come on," she says, "let's give you a hug."

Immediately I feel better. Much, much better. We stand there hugging each other. I say: "We're so lucky, some people are married who can't talk to each other." At the same time I'm slowly turning us round so I can see in the mirror which one of us it is she's giving a hug to. No question about it, it's me. What's more I look excellent. I look really pretty much together.

6

Odd synchronicity. SM says: "Very often when you're making your first contact with your inner stuff the inner stuff will keep, like, cropping up on the surface. The inner, which is timeless, right, tangles with the outer. The whole process is really bizarre and mystifying, but it shows in all sorts of weird coincidences."

I can't wait to tell her. "I'm glad you mentioned that. I've been having some very weird coincidences."

"Like what?"

"Like when I first went to ring you. I lifted the phone. No dial tone, but I could hear this person breathing. And then this horrendous crunch. 'What's going on?' I say. 'Oh so it's you, is it?' says a voice. Corny. 'That's Corny, isn't it? What the hell's going on?' 'Nothing much. I'm eating an onion.'"

"Who's Corny?" SM asks. She's looking all attentive.

"Corny's Cornelius. Dennis told Fiona about him. He's the character who does gold leaf. He's quite a nice bloke. Says he's a reincarnated Cathar!"

I'm thinking that'll amuse her, but not in the least. She's still looking attentive. In fact she's looking decidedly impressed. Maybe I know the right people.

"Does he?" she says, meaning: Does he indeed! "And who's Mr Caruso?"

I look at her. I say: "Hang about, I haven't mentioned Mr Caruso... Yet."

"Right," she says. "So who's Dennis?"

7

Bad Dream/Dennis. Wake at 4 am badly shaken. As usual I've not had a wink of sleep. The bed seems to be a raft. The water is inky black, full of wicked snappers. I can't make out whether I'm awake or not. I think: If this is our bed, Fiona should be here somewhere. I begin to feel around.

"Oh for God's sake not now. Do go to sleep."

The brush-off. That clinches it. She is, she's having an affair. I feel totally desperate. Suddenly I'm remembering my dream.

The dream: I'm in terrible danger. I'm walking the plank. I'm being prodded from behind by pirates with sticks. I look down. The water is mucky, like in the docks. On the surface hundreds of condoms. But there's the one place it's clear, about the size of a manhole. A shaft of clear water going down into a garden. I think, maybe I could dive down that shaft. I'm about to leap when in horror I draw back into the prodding sticks. There in the garden is Fiona walking arm in arm with a shadowy young man.

I say aloud: "If that doesn't prove it."

"I suppose you've had your exam dream again."

"No much worse."

"You don't mean it! Now go to sleep."

"I only wanted you to give me a hug."

This is true, but at the same time I feel I have contrived a subtle test. Her response will tell me finally whether or not she is having an affair.

"Alright. But then you go to sleep."

"Mummy," I say.

"What did you say?"

"I..." I hesitate. "I don't think I said anything very much."

Fiona shifts. I grab hold of her.

"Oh God, what time is it?"

"Very late." I say this with dire conviction.

Fiona sits up and switches on her bedside light. "Like what?"

"Like, well," I say "it's as good as after seven."

"Just don't tell me," she groans. Throws herself back and pulls a pillow over her head. So I have to shout.

"I've had a very bad dream. Very bad."

She lifts the corner of the pillow.

"Know something? You're beginning to drive me nuts. Come on then."

"You were under the sea in this garden walking arm in arm with this young, er... young, young..."

I try for all I'm worth to keep in touch with reality by remembering the night in the college bar I took a leg off Brian Telfont in the arm-wrestle. But no use, if I say "young man" it is, it's going to happen. I'm going to start to cry.

Fiona comes out from under the pillow. She sits up.

"What did he look like?"

"I couldn't see-ee-ee."

"You poor love, you are in a bad way, aren't you?"

"Mummy."

"What did you say?"

"I didn't say anything," I say definitely.

"You are, you're a poor love. You've been picking up something. Very odd and rather funny."

She closes her eyes and begins to laugh.

"You know Dennis?"

"Who's Dennis for Christ's sake?" I can't help it if my voice is a bit shrill.

"You know, Dennis. He does leather work and has come to live in the village. He wants to learn how to run a business. He's taken a monumental shine to Annabel."

"Oh, that Dennis." I begin to laugh in a silly way. Then I think:

What does she mean, wants to learn to run a business? As if that weren't something to be massively worried about.

"Annabel's not impressed. But the funny thing is he makes me go weak at the knees. I think I've got a crush on him. It's totally irrational. Like the one I had at school on Zoe Pendleton. It must be my time of life! Along with the hot flushes and feeling I'm not doing anything useful. It's ridiculous because he's really odd-looking. Not my type at all – except somewhere where he's got this look of you. Annabel and I both think so."

I say: "Thank you." And feel that in the circumstances I'm succeeding in being magnificent. Then I say: "Anyway what d'you mean, nothing useful?"

"Well I'm not. Sometimes I feel all I ever do is just fiddle around the house. I feel I'm wasting myself."

Everything is much worse than I imagined. If she thinks life's so boring then of course she's going to be having an affair. One's always reading about it – housing estates, the milkman. Or sometimes it's the plumber. I may have imagined she was having an affair – but I never supposed there would be a reason, let alone someone real at the back of it. Someone I might bump into, with an actual name, like Dennis. Who would like to run a business.

I say: "Okay, Okay, one thing at a time. We were talking about this, this whatsisname."

"Dennis."

"What do you mean, he looks like me?"

"The good-looking bits."

"You mean his good-looking bits."

"No, yours."

"Oh, so he's good-looking."

"No actually he's rather extraordinary-looking."

"I see. And he looks like me. Okay."

But inside I feel something tearing. I can see it beginning to flap like a black bin-liner in the wind. And at the same time a thought goes scuttling for cover: She feels she's wasting her time – next she'll be suggesting she takes over running the conservatory business. Probably in partnership with Dennis. And that'll be that.

Fiona is watching me. I realize I'm chewing my bottom lip.

"You're not by any small chance going to get all upset?" She's sounding irritable.

Irritable! At this moment in my life when I've virtually had it confirmed that my wife's having an affair... just when I could use a dose of her understanding blue eyes, here they are all fired-up and grey.

"Don't be ridiculous," I say, and manage to get to the bathroom before I have a really major breakdown.

8

Homespun. Annabel is coming out of the bathroom. This is her third week at the Tech – Diploma in Hotel Catering and Management. She leaves the house at quarter to eight on her moped. I notice her hair has changed again. At the end of the first week it was suddenly coming out in black spikes. This week it's softer, curly and yellow with a streak of orange.

I say: "Third week – into soup. Flavour of the month: tomato."

Gutsy performance that for a man who's staving off a complete collapse.

"Come on, dad – you wouldn't want us ringing for the yellow van."

She has, she's noticed.

She must have seen my expression because she calls back gaily from her bedroom. "Sorry dad, only joking."

I run into the bathroom and slam the door. The world may as well know how I'm feeling. Now what! I can't be alone for a moment. Look who's there in the mirror, all red-eyed and pouchy. It's too early in the day to face him. I go and collapse on the loo.

I'm thinking: From here they'll need to carry me out – when I notice I'm chewing my lower lip furiously. I realize what has happened. My eye is set on two words scratched in sinister childish hand in the top margin of the top magazine on the stool beside the loo.

"Luv Dennis."

I take a tight hold on myself and pick up the magazine. *Homespun.*

Contents: *Building a Fox-proof Coop, Assertiveness and the Feminine Mode,* Christ! *Goats: the Homoeopathic Approach.* I glance around the bathroom in acute anxiety. So this is what's been going on behind my back. Page after page and it's all happening locally. I reach the back cover: Small Ads, Members' Market, Skillswap Column, Wholeness and Personal Growth. I feel vaguely reassured – classified ads is me, mail order catalogues, anything like that. But Personal Growth? I'm into new territory. Hydrotherapy? African Dance as an Energetic Experience? Yes, I suppose it would be. Reflexology, Shamanistic Dance, Shiatsu, Feminine Mysteries. Column after column and all of it local. I read with a kind of queasy fascination. At the bottom of the penultimate column my eye sticks. The shortest of all entries.

SOROR MYSTICA. Tel: Langland 430.

I leap up and run out onto the landing.

"And I don't want him coming anywhere near this house," I shout.

Fiona and Annabel both open their doors.

"Who are you yelling at?"

"Damned if I know," I mutter, and run back into the bathroom.

A moment later Annabel's knocking on the door.

"Yes?" I say manfully.

"Dad, you know you were asking mum if there was someone who does gold leaf? Well Dennis says he knows this person."

9

Turn off the main road. Half a mile, past the farm with the green silo, over the little stone bridge, the first track on the left.

The directions are in Annabel's hand, dictated by... well, bully for Dennis.

There's white smoke coming out of the chimney in puffs, like it's Indians. Or a new Pope. The place is more of a shed than a house. It has a cover of what looks like kicking-board – that's it, a stable turned inside-out. On the grass outside the stable-door, piles of every sort of junk. At least three generators in bits. A heap of scrap metal. The dismantled sections of an old greenhouse the size of Crystal Palace. There's an odd vehicle parked beside the door – a kind of aerial pedalo with wings made of laminated paper, string and peacock feathers.

The door's open. I don't knock. Instead I shout: "Anyone at home?" From inside comes a double-barrelled grunt. Which I first interpret as "Piss off!" But then decide could, with a mouthful, have been "Come in."

A lank, tanned fellow in his thirties, with a lick of black hair, and these black eyes which seem to flash every now and then with a sort of summer lightning. The place has all those wholesome painter smells. Turps and linseed and spirit-gum. As well as other smells – for instance there's a line of rabbit skins drying above the stove, and on shelves and benches and the table there are so many jars and pots and beakers that in one of them somewhere, something has to be a little bit off.

I say: "I'm looking for Cornelius."

Finally, just when I'm beginning to think I must have been chewing my bottom lip and he's taking the piss, he stops chewing.

He removes something from his mouth and says: "Just fixing me up with a couple of new choppers – means you need to take a gum impression, right?"

"What you make your own teeth?" I say. "Not in gold!"

He tilts and half turns his head so he's looking at me out the top corners of his eyes. At length he says in a voice that seems to echo out of a catacomb: "The viscous gold which is called red gum and with which the three earthy natures are tinted."

"Good grief!" I say, and snatch both hands over my heart. "What in God's name was that?"

From outside the door behind me had come what I would describe as an awful cry of lamentation.

He says: "That in God's name is possibly a peacock."

"You keep peacocks?"

He closes one eye, turns his head a little to the side and with the other eye cases me as if to indicate that my question is indiscreet.

"If you live in a palace," he says, "you have a peacock."

I choose to ignore this, though the way my heart's knocking I feel an apology would be in order. I say: "Someone said you do gold leaf."

"Beat it? Lay it? Or do you mean invent it?"

"I mean you know how to stick it on. I have a client, Mr Caruso..."

"Caruso?"

"You know Mr Caruso?"

Corny is scratching his chin with one forefinger, and is examining me as if in final deliberation over my application to join his Masonic Lodge. Suddenly the forefinger moves, is pointing to something above the door behind me. There, in a kind of cup on a shelf, is a, well it's either a coconut or an ostrich egg. Only it's gleaming gold.

I think: You've just done yourself a favour, lad.

10

Difficult morning. Something tiresome about Jennie always being punctual. This morning she's punctual and jumpy. Probably the curate playing up. She's been engaged to him as long as we've known her (three years).

One wouldn't call her altogether shapeless, because she does have a here-and-there bulkiness, as well as the pale, mucousy look. Asked how she's feeling she tends to say: "It doesn't seem to want to come to anything."

I say: "What you should try Jennie is a..." and then have to look suddenly preoccupied, "...is a couple of aspirins and plenty of fresh air."

She sniffs. If I'd said what I was intending to say she'd have come out in prickly heat. I'd been going to say: "You should try a weekend of African Dance as an Energetic Experience."

Today she's making a statement, wearing for a change her severe brown skirt, immaculately pleated, as well as the blue chiffon blouse, which would be audacious if it weren't for the gathered frilly bit down the front. This does create a modest question. In vacant moments I have found myself exploring the question, but only from a statistical standpoint. The other day Fiona said: "You should watch it, there's more to our Jennie than you, my bright boy, have any inkling of." Maybe, but she's a lousy typist.

Today she's even worse because she's all on edge. Keeps clicking her tongue irritably. I think: Maybe she's picking up something from me. I'm on edge.

I've been putting the final touch to the individual design for the Besseldon Manor conservatory – plenty of hanging-down bits to carry the gold leaf. I glance at Jennie – what on earth is she up to? Now she's begun chewing her lower lip. That does it. Right, this is where I claim back the power-seat – do my Burt Lancaster in The Sweet Smell of Success impersonation.

"Jennie," I say, "get Caruso on the line. Quick."

As Jennie picks up the phone she gives an insolent sigh and me a worn-out look which says: "Oh no, not again!" She dials and passes me the phone.

Burp-burp, burp-burp... and then Callas's usual suave recitative: "The Director of Besseldon Manor is away on extended business. If you would care to state your message, name and telephone number we will be pleased..."

I yell: "Blackguard!" Jennie jumps out of her three layers of Vitamin E cream. "Extended business in the commodities market of the Orient, the swine!" I growl. She snatches for her Tipp-ex, fumbles the bottle and it's all over her skirt. I take her down to the kitchen to get her sorted out.

Fiona, bless her, is warm and business-like and insists on doing the mopping up. I seem to feel there's something that needs explaining. "It's Tipp-ex." I stress this several times. "That's all it is. I was down the other end of the room."

"Oh," says Fiona in a jolly, conversational way, "what were you doing there?"

I'm suddenly seeing red.

"What do you mean, what was I doing? I wasn't doing anything. I told you, I was down the other end of the room."

We have a tense silence.

"I think that's got the worst of it off," Fiona says. Now what's she doing? She's struggling to get out of her blue jumper. She's having a hot flush.

"It was only Tipp-ex," I say. For some reason I'm now feeling considerably agitated. I need some air.

"Not a bad day," I say. "I'm off for a walk... I mean gardening. There's a lot needs doing in the garden."

But outside the door I hesitate. I think I've heard Jennie say: "He's always been so considerate, so... so predictable."

I think: Well, thank you. Thanks very much.

Then I hear Fiona say: "I'm sure it's nothing. He's just going through an unpredictable phase."

I think: That's a mistake, leaving those two together. They'll talk. Jennie's sure to talk. Cuckolded by Dennis. It will be all over the district.

I run back in. Fiona is fanning herself with *The Observer*.

"Come on, Jennie," I say. "We must get back to work."

11

I'm thinking: Jennie's got to go. If she were to get hold of this it would be worse than *The Argus* – the whole district would know, including the Church. Oh my God, and the Rotary! I watch her from the other end of the room. She's daubing the entire page with Tipp-ex again. She sniffs. This time the sniff runs into three syllables and sounds ominously liquid. She isn't, is she, going to cry? Yes she is.

"What's up?"

"I seem to be picking up a lot of bad energy. I don't feel you really want me. It's making me make mistakes."

"Don't be ridiculous. It's this thing you think's wrong with you. You're a degree or two under. I expect it's decided to come to something. I think you should go home."

"I thought that's what you were thinking."

"Jennie, you're not yourself. Come on now, I'll drive you."

Fiona looks up as we hurry through the kitchen.

"Where are you two off to?"

"Us? We're just popping back to Jennie's place. I mean, I'm running her home. You're not feeling too good are you Jennie?"

Jennie sniffs in a rhetorical way which I know is prelude to some sort of emotional outburst. I say: "There, there, poor old you." And hurry her down the passage.

We drive in silence. I look at her sidelong. As I do so she puts her right hand fingers on her chestbone and swallows.

"I don't think I should come again, do you?"

"Jennie you're being melodramatic. The situation is bound to improve."

"Which situation?" You could say she merely breathes this, but actually it is more of a dry little death-rattle. I think: That's a really mischievous question.

"I'm not referring to a specific situation. I mean the general situation. I should have thought that was obvious."

But this doesn't console her. She sobs: "And I always thought of you as being so wonderfully calm. I mean, before you got into this unpredictable phase."

"Oh shut up!" I say. Which I'd have thought was fairly predictable.

I drop her at her mother's place. She can't easily say goodbye because she's so busy dabbing various bits of her face with a tissue. As she runs up the path I call after her.

"Take it easy now. We'll look forward to seeing you in the morning."

I'm quite surprised when I realize I've sounded genuinely warm. I take a look at myself in the mirror. It's me. I'm not looking too bad.

12

Turning into the drive I have this clear vision. I wouldn't really know a vision if I saw one, but this one's so clear it's like a blackout. I slam on the brakes. When I open my eyes I find I need to reverse – the front of the car's in the rhododendrons. The image has come and gone in a trice, like the impact of light when one walks into a wall. It takes some time to come to. The image is of me finding Fiona in bed with somebody. A single frame, very vivid and indefinite. Somebody – I can't say more than that. Though I do of course have my suspicions.

I walk into the house whistling. I'm whistling 'Kiss Me In The Rain,' which is understandable. For some reason I feel whistling is a sensible precaution. I don't walk upstairs, I walk straight into the kitchen.

Fiona is leaning over the Rayburn stirring something in that methodical 'I'm-on-top-of-everything' way she picked up from her father. Though not as cool as she'd have me think. Maybe she's merely hot from the stove, but it looks to me as if she's having another hot flush.

"Look who's here," she says.

I've wondered a lot since whether she was addressing me or Dennis.

Dennis is sitting at the kitchen table which is laid for lunch for three.

"Hi, hi there, hullo," he says. Can one imagine a clearer confession of guilt?

He's wearing a long smock-like khaki parka and grey trawlerman's socks. As I look at him I feel myself begin to chew my bottom lip.

"Looked by with a book for Annabel," says Dennis.

On the table beside him is a small seamy-looking book in a brown paper cover. Brown paper.

He's picking up my feelings, seems to realize he owes an explanation.

"My favourite book. I keep it in brown paper. To protect it."

I suddenly feel tremendously agitated. I've walked in on something. "Why three places?" That proves it, whatever it is, beyond any discussion.

"I've suggested Dennis stops," Fiona says. "He can eat Jennie's lunch."

"I see." The way I say this it sounds like an accusation. It is. No one in his right mind is going to tolerate someone who's probably having an affair with his wife, bringing stuff into the house in brown paper covers.

"Right," I say. "I'll see she gets that. I'll put it in her room."

Before he can blink I've picked up the book and made off with it to the office. I shut the door behind me, grit my teeth and open the pages. I'm trembling so much I can hardly see the words.

It's *The Odyssey*.

13

Lunch in silence. Except for the phenomenal noise that Dennis achieves with the air-intake transfer of soup from spoon to mouth. Finally I feel bound to take a look at him. I think: The only bit that isn't really peculiar is the nose. I'm wondering whether that could be the good-looking bit. I begin with the fingers of my left hand to feel the shape of my nose. Dennis looks at me and looks away. He seems totally unprepared for his next spoon of soup. Fiona fetches him kitchen tissues and a j-cloth. When he's mopped up he suddenly remembers he's needed in his workshop. He has to see a man about a belt. He looks at Fiona.

"Really great," he says. He ignores me.

I think: I see.

So I go after him with: "This Cornelius, how did you come to get acquainted with such a resourceful chap?"

Dennis says: "We craftspeople tend to stick together."

"Ah yes," I say. "His whole place did reek of glue. Rabbit-skin of course."

14

Gardening. The slack in the office does leave more time for the garden. Gardening is calming and an opportunity to think through any problems. Today it seems to be bringing up a lot of aggression in me.

I yell: "Caruso, you fat little shit!"

I take off my jacket, spit on my hands and shout: "No, this time you'll kindly listen to me."

And begin to fork furiously.

15

Teatime. I'm in the kitchen washing my hands. I'm still muttering away.

Someone's coming. I instinctively adopt a pathetic 'look-at-me-I'm-wounded' expression. Quite right, it's Fiona.

I say: "Love, whatever's the matter?"

She's trying to smile but is looking all of a flush, and is crying. Fiona doesn't cry easily. Wonderful and warm, but she can be very calm, and where other people would be crying she tends to smile and say: "It's nothing, I'll be alright in a minute."

She says: "I feel I'm wasting my life. I'm not doing anything."

What does she mean, 'I'm not doing anything'? I never said she was doing anything.

I say: "You can do anything." Which makes me think: She's going to bring it up again – my record with the conservatory business. She wants to run the show.

She says: "I'm being really stupid."

"Of course you're not."

I put my arms round her. I think: We're so close it's uncanny. We always have been.

I say: "Love, just tell me what's up."

"I know it's nothing, just my time of life."

That's when I know. What's up is her choosing this moment to make the final declaration about her and Dennis.

I say: "It's about you and Dennis, isn't it?"

She takes a startled breath. I think: How, after all these years, can she think I wouldn't know?"

"No, it's not," she says. "It's about you and Jennie."

Me and Jennie?

"Me and Jennie!"

"The way you just suddenly rushed off with her. You were gone for hours. This afternoon, I seemed to well, I seemed to get to thinking."

"What, this afternoon? This afternoon *I* seemed to get to thinking. All afternoon. About you and Dennis."

We look at each other and begin to laugh.

"I love you," I say. "I really do seem to love you very, very much."

"I love you."

We're giving each other this big hug.

"Now what's up?" Fiona says.

"Just that..." I thought I'd get something cleared up once and for all, "you didn't did you? I mean when you were alone with Jennie, tell her about you and Dennis?"

"Of course not."

I laughed. "And about me and Jennie – you didn't, of course, tell Dennis?"

She looks startled. "Why, what's there to tell?"

"Nothing."

Fiona is heating up again. "Then why did you have to come back whistling like that?"

"I thought something was going on. I was keeping calm."

"Yes, but you rush off with Jennie and come back whistling 'Kiss Me In The Rain.'"

"That's what you keep whistling. I picked it up from you. You were whistling it outside the linen cupboard when I... when I thought..."

We begin to laugh. Suddenly I'm happier than I've been for months. We give each other another big cuddle. Heaven!

"Oi, oi!"

It's Annabel. She's walked in the door.

"Right in the middle of peak family viewing. Disgusting."

"In this day and age my girl, you should be grateful if your mother and father are even on speaking terms."

What's up with our child? She's looking radiant. She comes and joins the hug. Burrows right into the middle. Over her head I look at Fiona. She smiles at me. She looks unbelievably young and happy.

"Mummy..." I say.

Fiona looks at me in surprise and then puts her hand over her mouth as if to stop some cat getting out of a bag.

I say: "Don't look at me – I didn't say anything."

Annabel says: "Guess what, I met this gorgeous fella. He was next to me in the dinner-queue. David. Into industrial drawing or something."

Fiona says: "So we have David to thank for this little demonstration of love."

Annabel rolls her eyes wickedly at the ceiling.

I think: Christ. I hope she doesn't start bringing this one home. I've enough on my plate with Dennis. I do, I feel really threatened.

"Oh, and guess who I ran into on my way home. Gawky Dennis."

"Careful. I told dad we think he looks like him."

"He does. No he doesn't. Well only in parts. Guess what he said? He said: 'Your mum's a really gorgeous lady.' Mum I think he really fancies you."

"And what does he think of me?" I manage this almost without emotion.

"Come on dad, he wouldn't be about to fancy you!"

He wouldn't, wouldn't he? Right. That proves it.

16

10pm – I'm meditating. Imperative I get a decent night's sleep. I feel there's a dickens of a lot at stake on this meditation, and it hasn't got off to a good start. There's so much racket inside my head (backchat with the likes of Dennis and Cornelius, and messages from Caruso on the answerphone, as well as speculative badinage with this new boy David). I have to raise my voice to get Soahum hearing.

The snag I find with meditation is that when one's in the pink it's pretty straightforward – but when one really needs it, for instance when one doesn't know what the hell's going on behind one's back, then one would be as well off counting sheep.

I try to concentrate on my breathing. Sounds ragged – as if my plugs need a clean. Very unsettling. But I stick with it. After a time I feel I'm beginning to win. I have to suppress my excitement. I am, I'm beginning to win. I think: Maybe I'm on the point of a breakthrough. This could be it, the big conversion experience. People say it does often happen when one's at one's wits' end. You don't get to feel much lower than I have today. Yes that's it. I feel it coming, I'm about to make it. I'll show everybody – Telfont,

Caruso, the lot. Why, I might even mount a hostile take-over of Besseldon Manor and open an ashram – a bit of poojah in the conservatory. The idea brings a lot of peace...

Suddenly this light cuts clean through my brain, a laser through sponge. I feel the warmth spread as my grey matter begins to haemorrhage. And then it goes black. I think: There, it's happened. I shall probably find I've been converted. I'll probably find I'm a Buddhist or something. I expect I'm blind. I open my eyes. Everything's fine.

So what does all this add up to, I'm thinking, when... when, when it begins to happen again – the dark rising from below the flimsy floor, the vacuum of it drawing me in, the hollow pain, a groan silent on the intaken breath. I clench my fists. But I don't think this time I'll be able to hold it down.

Suddenly I'm running. Through the kitchen, across the hall, into the sitting-room. I grab the telephone.

Burp-burp, burp-burp... "Mr Caruso is on extended business in the Far..."

That's done it. I put down the receiver, snatch it up again, am about to redial when... there is, there's somebody on the line. I can hear the breathing.

"What's going on?" I say.

"So it's you." I know the voice. "Hardly surprising, I was about to ring you. That would confirm that the way is open, and you're one who doesn't need to be told, *Aurum nostrum non est aurum vulgi.*"

It's Cornelius.

I say: "Hullo, yes, it's me. What the hell do you want?"

"You're into gold, aren't you? I was reading something of gold, and experienced instruction to run it past you."

I want to tell him I'm not in the mood, that as a matter of fact he's caught me at a moment when I'm extremely agitated. But somehow I can't get it out.

He says; "You still there? Fine. Okay, now listen to this: 'Build a temple of stone, having neither beginning nor end in its construction. Let it have within it a spring of pure water glittering like the sun. A serpent lies before the entry. Seize him and sacrifice him. Skin him and, taking his flesh and bones, separate his parts (on those three words he lays a chilling stress). Then, reuniting the members with the bones at the entry of the temple, make of them a stepping stone, mount thereon and enter. You will find there what you seek. For the priest, the man of copper, whom you see seated in the spring gathering his colour, do not regard him as a man of copper; for he has changed the colour of his nature and become a man of silver. If you wish, after a little time you will have him as a man of gold.'"

Silence.

"You there?"

I can't trust myself to reply. I know its silly but there are tears running down my face. And I haven't understood a single word. I put down the receiver. When I've pulled myself together I pick it up again. There's no dialling tone, just the sound of faint breathing.

"For Christ's sake Corny, will you get off my line!"

"Who are you calling?" asks a woman's voice, deadpan, a brown husky colour.

I daren't say a word.

"Hullo... are you there? This is Langland 430."

17

SM doesn't say anything for a time. She seems absorbed in what she's doing, nimbling a corn dolly – a spiral plait. Then in a matter of fact way she says: "That's really amazing."

I'm not sure what she's referring to, Cornelius or the coincidence.

"Amazing?" I say.

She looks at me, her eyes like a total eclipse, looks back at her work.

I say: "What are you making?"

She says: "Another weird coincidence. The Suffolk Coil, it's the circumambulatio – the going round in circles before the real work begins. Alright, since nothing's likely now to prevent you from coming nicely in pieces, I'm prepared to work with you. When would you like to begin?"

And then she does it again – wipes her nose on her sleeve.

2
SEPARATIO

18

The road becomes a lane becomes a track. Where the track becomes a path, there's a place to park. Then something I didn't notice the first time: Stone Cottage – the letters dotted with a hot poker point in a driftwood plank.

It's a quarter of a mile down the path. I'm early. We agreed five pm. I'm in a calm phase. I think: Lets just go over this again...

Come to think of it, not so calm.

Golden afternoon. The light's liquid gold: everything, even the grass, dipped in it. Fruit everywhere, in startling clarity – sloes like damsons, hips, blackberries, rosaries of briony. I think: I must be barmy – best if I just run along home. That does it. Home, Fiona, with or without Dennis. Wide open again, coming to bits. My teeth start to chatter. I think: You are, you're in a real pickle, not a marble left to your name...

Then I think: Yes, and that's why you're here, remember? How did she put it? 'Nicely in pieces.'

I start down the path. Something materializes behind me. It's, it's the one magpie! It follows me down the path, jumping from twig to twig, yelling obscenities.

19

The cottage seems to breathe through its open door. Breathing in lavender, breathing out cider vinegar. I'm about to knock when I hear someone coming. That does it – my face begins to leap with twitches. I want to swat them. Christ, what's this! Oh I see, it's a goat. It stands in the doorway, head on one side, its mouth threaded with a carrot, and two inspired loony eyes asking what I want. I want the hell out of it. The goat stops chewing. I'll swear it's begun to frown.

It shrugs, and walks back into the kitchen.

I think: Where is she? She's late. This is most unprofessional.

20

The magpie sits on the roof. Wipes its beak on its dress-shirt before it takes another close look at me. A butterfly, I think a painted lady, persistently tries to settle on my forehead. A muscovy duck the size of an emu is taking bludgeoning pecks at my shoelace. My irritation's getting out of hand. Suddenly it becomes a jigging swarm of gnats with scimitar stings. I lash out. The voice says, "I can't stand much more of this." A frantic voice – presumably mine, though I don't recognize it.

"Sounds encouraging."

I say: "I beg your pardon?"

She's about four feet away, must have come from round the back. I think: So now she's got herself pregnant. Really, that's so unprofessional – then I see she's carrying runner beans in the scoop of her white starched apron.

"A good time to start work."

"What, you mean now?"

"I mean when you can't stand being where you are any longer is the time to move on."

She looks like a colour illustration on a Victorian seed catalogue. Green and crimson Laura Ashley flouncing out from under the apron, and her hair with an auburn tinge.

SM says: "Go on in. The flies don't come in the house." Very little expression, yet even with just that last statement there's more power flying around than meets the ear. I go on in.

Seems that downstairs there's only the kitchen. Whitewash and pine, slate floor, low ceiling, pine table, open shelves, piles of jars, bottles, fruit, veg, utensils (most of them with wooden handles). Under the table, kittens, a chicken with umpteen ducklings, a couple of rabbits, the goat of course (in fact it's a kid) flat out in the armchair. The whole place alive. The only dead thing is the grey threadbare skin rug in front of the Rayburn.

I think: Don't remember any of this. I suppose it is the same place.

"Something to drink?"

"Please."

"Peppermint? Red Zinger? Vervaine?"

"Red er...," I take a gamble – it sounds like the strong stuff.

"Zinger," she says.

I'm looking round for the source of the light. There's more light in this room than there is outside in the golden day. Out of a side-chink in my eye I see the mat get up from in front of the Rayburn and slope off out of the door.

It's a damn great Irish wolfhound.

21

SM's First Message. I'm sitting on the arm of the goat's chair sipping my Red Zinger. SM quits slicing runner beans, wipes her hands on her apron, fetches a small block of notepaper and begins to write. After a couple of minutes she tears off the sheet, comes and hands it to me. I look up at her. I feel a complicated warmth and dependence – I think to do with her being young enough to be my daughter.

"Mummy," I say. I didn't mean to say that.

She widens her eyes (at this moment they're gem green), puts her forefinger emphatically to her lips, holds it there a long time, then nods to indicate I should read the note. It's written in a rounded girlish hand, the 'I's dotted with little circles.

Outside, you were broken in hundreds of places. Behind you in the spinney there was this big neglected person. He was sweating a lot and smelt rotten. In the doorway was a kind of brilliant angel. You didn't see him because he was in your shadow. Everywhere you look is in shadow so long as you are unaware of your shadow behind you. Right? You can't even see who you're wrestling with. Actually, you're in quite a tangle. Tangles aren't difficult to undo once one's found where the string begins.

I look up at her. Her eyes are this green question: "Get it?"

I nod. Can't think why because I sure as hell don't get any of it. She takes the note from my fingers, goes and opens the firebox of the Rayburn and chucks it in.

"The Separatio," she says, as if that's going to explain everything. "You can't get it together, your real self I mean, until this unreal self has come to bits. Separation, now do you see?"

Through the bustles of Laura Ashley, SM first locates, then scratches her bottom.

22

I say: "I mean, how do I... how does one begin?"

She says: "You don't. If you were to begin you'd begin in the wrong place. You'd go for what you saw as the problem. The problem's never the problem, just as the solution is always the answer to the next question but one."

"I don't have that much time. I mean..." my voice is so much of a bleat it sounds as if I'm taking the piss out of the goat. "... I wouldn't be here if I knew what the hell to do."

She turns and looks at me, still drying the inside of a jar. "You don't. You let him begin."

I look round the room uneasily. They're all watching me.

"Him?" I ask.

"So you've not met up. Listen, can you hear him breathing?"

I listen. I can hear the Rayburn kind of breathing. I can hear something else breathing, like the cottage. I notice the goat has again stopped chewing and is looking at me with intense interest. I shake my head.

"Alright. Can you hear you breathing?"

I realize then I've been holding my breath. So I start to breathe. Yes, I hear that – very ragged and breathless. A very distressed sort of breathing. I nod.

"Right. So your breathing's stopping you hearing his breathing. Let him do the breathing."

I think: Christ!

"What, my breathing?"

"No, the breathing."

Suddenly I've taken or rather been taken by a breath so slow and so deep my ribcage cricks like a whicker-chair. I'm not breathing any more. I've my mouth shut. I think: If I don't breathe I'm going to peg out. I feel oddly calm about this – maybe because I don't seem to be pegging out. Then I realize she's right – there's breathing going on. Almost imperceptible, the in-out, out-in changes are entirely imperceptible, but evidently adequate. I am, I'm being breathed.

The goat starts to chew again. I have this daft feeling the whole room's been in suspense, wondering: will he ever twig? I look at SM. She's crying a little. No she isn't, she's dicing an onion.

"Well met," she says. "So now you can begin. Some people it takes much longer."

I'm tempted to glow, but then, "Hang on," I say. "I still don't know, I mean where do I begin?"

"He'll know." She manages to say this with the sort of patience that doesn't in any way imply the existence of impatience. "Since you now trust him you leave it to him."

"I do, do I, trust him?"

"Well it wasn't you breathing just now, was it?"

I shake my head.

"See, you've just, like, trusted him with your life."

I must have twitched or made a face or something.

"You stopped breathing, you allowed him to take over. If you can trust him with your life you can trust he'll know where to begin. Right?"

Her voice bustles along deftly, like a district nurse redoing somebody's bandage.

"Right." Certainly can't think of anything else to say. Except, "Er, by the way, who is he, I mean exactly?"

"Exactly... he's you." She says this as if it were the most obvious thing in the world, and then glances at the goat and raises both eyebrows as much as to say... actually I prefer not to think what she was going to say. Then she says: "So. In that cupboard beside the mangle – mattress and cushions. Get them comfy on the floor."

"Mum..." Actually I'm not sure I even started to say whatever I was about to say because this sounded more of an excited, or maybe terrified squeak. I don't have the nerve to look so I'll never know whether she noticed.

23

The wolfhound has vacated the pitch – he must know the form. I set the mattress and cushions in front of the friendly Rayburn, and then make myself comfortable on my back. SM is slicing the runners.

I'm exasperated. What's going on? Nothing's happening. Nobody's doing a blind thing. I'm straining to convince myself I should let *him* handle it. But can't help wondering what business it is of his, even if he is a dead-ringer for me – that's supposing there is or was any business in the first place. I'm becoming really very agitated. I'm gnawing so ravenously at my lower lip I seem intent on swallowing my chin. Suddenly the black bin liners are blowing... I'm being served notice of what Fiona is up to with me out of the house.

"It's ridiculous," I cry out to SM or the goat or whoever cares, "because really we do, we trust each other implicitly."

The telephone is ringing over by the door. The room is blazingly alight and airy. SM doesn't make a move, even though there was never a phone rang with such jarring urgency.

I think: That's for me – that's the fateful message. That's Caruso, calling from Penang.

I'm so worked up I roll on my side and begin hugging my knees. The phone stops ringing and leaves a silence as shrill as a kettle. I can't bear it. I've missed an imperative opportunity. Someone was trying to get hold of me and now...

I shout: "Why can't someone answer the bloody phone?"

SM says: "Phone? You heard a phone? Someone must be trying to get through to you."

"Ay..." I say.

I think: I beg your pardon!

"Ay... ay... ay..." I say, each syllable coming away with a grunt as if I've been kicked in the stomach. "Ay... Ayah, ay-ayah, ay-ayah. Ah...AYAH."

I think: So that's who it is, it's Ayah.

"Ayah," I say.

24

SM says: "Ah yes, born in India."

" Following the flag," I say as if standing to attention. I need us to move on from Ayah. "My mother I mean. My dad was a hell of an army man – plenty of pips."

SM looks at me carefully. She slides her head to one side. For an instant her eyes darken to umber. She closes one eye. "Plenty of pips," she says in what I would term a portentous manner. "I see. So now tell me, who is Ayah?"

I open my mouth to say: "How the devil should I know!" when I hear me intone, as if to state an awful reality, "Ayah is Ayah, right?"

SM approves of that, nods as if I'm at last getting the hang of it.

"You're in luck," she says. "Nutricia Nigra: the Black Nurse. All the way from the East."

"I suppose something to do with the Empire." Well, it seemed an intelligent thing to say.

SM definitely snorts, and then says darkly, "So the Empire fights back. Prepare yourself for the revenge. Ayah will get you sorted."

I'd swear she laughed at that. But when I check her expression I realise it may have been the goat. In fact I would say SM looks entirely vacant as she steps over me to slide a preserving pan of bean chutney onto the Rayburn. Then she says: "Maybe this Ayah's one end of the string. So now what do you do?"

"I let him handle it... of course."

"Him? Or do you perhaps mean her?"

I'm thinking: This is unreal. How do I know I'm seventeen inches long, flat on my back, which is not what I want, and strong enough to tackle the whole universe? Red Zinger powerful.

I let out a panther hiss to prove it. Kssss. Kssss. The sound scorches the room, it's like the breath of a blowlamp in the long jungle raffia.

"Kssss, Ayah Ayah."

My teeth in her throat – no sweat. I will in a minute – Ker-rist! – I'll mumble her throat. I'm growling now. I can smell her, a kind of stale-butter, cardamom-tasting pastry smell. Her shadow's enormous, a black-out big as a mountain, between me and the light. Between me and guess who... mummy. She is she's between me and my mummy. As if that isn't something to raise the roof about.

"Let it out," SM says busily – she's at the sink washing chutney jars.

"Ow... ow... ow." It's an unthinkable thing to have done. Cut me off. What is there could hurt more than that? They've cut me off from fucking everything. I'm left bald. I hurt everywhere like it's where I'm cut off, like the end of your finger or your prick – absolutely raw-nerved raw. The very slightest touch hurts unthinkably everywhere. The only way to get this pain across is to scream, not out from your tongue but from every sensitive bit – like one was a bucket of water screaming. Or else one could black out completely.

I am, I'm exhausted. Finally I manage to say, "Perhaps you would kindly tell me what that was all about."

SM says: "How would I know? I don't recall ever being circumcised."

26

The Chutney. I see, I say dreamily. I'm lying on my back looking up at the beams and the strings of drying basil. I feel I've come round after anaesthetic. SM busies past to stir the chutney.

"Like, it's an operation," she says.

"How do you know these things?" I notice there's more than a touch of ardour in my expression. She ignores this, blows on a wooden spoonful from the pan, tastes it.

"Mmmm," she says.

I'm getting agitated again. This attention to chutney is frivolous. In the present context – which is me on the floor in pieces.

I say: "So what does one do about it?"

"Nothing. Just breathe and wait while the pot boils and bubbles. Let the cooking do the cooking."

She licks a label and sticks it on a jar.

27

I let him do the breathing.

Fear comes shuffling back. Ayah's around. No centre to her, she's like a black steam room.

"Who's there?"

My voice is a shock, tells me I'm terrified. The blinds are flapping, letting the light come in gusts. A monkey bounds across the tin roof. Monkeys... of course, it's the monkeys!

"Who's there?" A boy's voice. "Who's there?"

Nobody.

There's nobody anywhere.

No mummy. She's gone out. By which I'm meaning, she's buggered off... just when I really need her, when I'm... when I'm... The panther in the empty room begins to growl. The bitch, this time she is going to have to say sorry.

28

I'm still not sure what happened in the cupboard.

I say: "I think maybe I shall have to go back in the cupboard."

SM says: "Well, why not? Come out when you're ready."

Her voice is an interruption. I snarl at her but she's not the least put out. I settle myself back in the cupboard. Not the cupboard beside the mangle – this is some sort of other dimension cupboard. In here the scent's clear, a mixture of woman and something waiting to be washed and violet talc. I make a slurping noise with my lips and tongue as if I'm enjoying the soup. Everything is just as I want it – secure, warm and definitely sexy.

Know what? I'm wearing somebody's green knickers. So much so I raise my head to see. No, I'm not really wearing them, it's just this strong feeling that I have.

Then I hear the steps. Coming up the stairs.

Along the passage.

Into the bedroom.

Uh uh, I know what's going to happen, though can't this moment exactly remember.

I think: this time I'm going to look, I'm going to see who it is.

Wham. I'm being picked up by the scruff. I'm tummy down over somebody's knee.

WOW, WOW, WOW.

I don't believe it, he's laying into me. I will, I'll kill him for this. Anyway what's so unforgivable about wearing a pair of green knickers?

29

Suddenly the fear is coming away in this delicious painful weeping grief.

I say: "Ow, ow, oh, how did they get it wrong?"

I suppose it is me saying this. I mean there's no one else it could be.

SM says: "Did they get it wrong?"

She has this knack of saying two things at once. For instance, what she also says is: "Did they get it wrong?"

I hear me say: "They weren't there... Ow! They weren't there... and I bleedin' well loved them."

Astonishing. I'm actually feeling the love. It's excruciating.

SM says: "What's the problem?"

"They – don't – need – my – love." It's like saying, "Ow, ow, ow, ow, ow."

"Hey," I say, sitting up. "If they've buggered off how can I love them? O love, no me. It's the end of me. It means... Christ... you see what this means?"

I'm sitting there. Seventeen inches, seventeen feet... I've no idea. I can feel the blaze of me. How do I ever explain?

I gasp: "That's all I am, was, am, was, am... this love."

"Stay with it," says SM.

I sink back on the mattress in a glow of fiery certainty. I'm able to breathe again. Or someone is. After what I've been through I need a sleep. I settle down to a sweet, clear, power-nap.

30

Vervaine. I say: "What's this stuff do for you?"

"Vervaine, holy herb." She smiles at me in that way of hers. It's as if she were smiling round the back of her head. She picks up a book called *Grandmother's Secrets* and reads: "Sorcerers lose their senses at the mention of this herb. For they say that those who are rubbed with it will obtain all they ask, and that it will cure fevers and cause a person to love another and, in short, that it cures all illnesses and more besides."

Snaps the book shut and looks at me with one eyebrow up. Eyes grass green, like one of grandmother's secrets.

"Sounds the ticket," I mumble – and take a good gulp.

31

SM's Second Message. The day's in golden decline. A blackbird singing, the centre of dreamy, panoramic attention. SM goes out of the door with a washing-up bowl of scraps, the animals in a file behind.

"Boukie-boukie-boukie," she calls.

I've been lying on this mattress for ever. There's no hurry. But I've a pressing need to talk.

As SM comes in the door I say "Yes, but what's all this to do with me and Fiona and... (I was going to say Dennis) ...and that crook Caruso? You don't realize. I'm in a hellish fix."

She doesn't reply. I think: Silly question. She sits at the table and reaches for her notebook.

As she writes I have an uncanny tingling sensation in the back of my head. At the same time I'm experiencing an almighty anger. I find I'm thinking: Anyway I was only into the knickers to feel near her. If she hadn't kept swanning off with him, leaving me to be interfered with by Ayah, I'd have been out of that cupboard years ago.

SM passes me the note.

You've got there – the baby is the experience of the father and mother's love. That's what those two made, remember? They made love.

I look up.

I say: "Why do you need to write this?"

"If I say it, it's me saying it to you. If you see it, you see it as it is. That way it's truer!"

I nod in a dazed way, and begin to read the rest of the note.

The child is love but it has to experience this to become assured of it. If it doesn't experience its father's love and its mother's love, its experience of love is incomplete. It experiences itself as an incomplete person.

I look up at her. She's occupied, putting the elastic bands over the cellophane tops to the chutney – such an intense and yearning expression on her face I feel sudden pain for her. My question goes out of my mind. Instead I say inanely: "Doesn't that go for just about all of us? Who's going to help us all get off the hook? Or hooked back up again?"

She looks at me a long time. I have the odd sensation that the room's light, which is now more of a gloaming, a deep golden green, is spilling out of her eyes. When she does speak it's as if she gently blows the words at me: "Ayah, of course."

32

Here it is again, the surrounding brown horror. But this time it can't dent my anger. I hiss between my teeth, begin to growl. The rage is grand.

Ha, back in the cupboard, waiting. This time I'm ready for him. Here come the footsteps. The door opens, in comes the light, and it's straight into the beating. I laugh – now I know who I am I can soak up any amount of this.

SM says: "Go on, face him."

"Piss off," I hiss.

As I turn, as I look up, I see this harrowed darkened face. And there, reaching away behind like that line of royal ghosts Macbeth met in the cave, is the dim ancestral chain of cause and effect. I can see them quite clearly, can even smell them. Heroic fathers, macho grandfathers coming each in his time wearing his medals, flashing his pips, to fix this bit of him he's stashed away in the spare room cupboard – that's programmed him to the moment he finds himself drawn up the stairs, along the passage, into the spare room and... wham, wham, wham. As if this were his opportunity to get shot of it. Where he does his bit, thrashes the boy till he knows what's what. The effeminate secret's safe with him. He'll not now be likely to spill the beans. Not ever.

"So that's what you thought, eh dad? Oh dear, oh dear."

I hold him. It's his cupboard more than it's my cupboard. I am holding him. Ow... the heart-cover rips, and the hot stuff is pouring out down into the stomach-sump. Begins filling me up.

33

I say: "What's this for God's sake?" I'm holding this big roly-poly cushion in my arms.

SM says: "You tell me. You seemed to be looking for something to hug?"

"Oh," I say sheepishly. "This... this is my dad."

She doesn't blink.

I say: "Know something? I get the feeling I'm doing him a favour."

"Go on," she says.

"It's like I'm letting him off the hook."

She smiles invisibly. There are shadows in the room now, the light is thick green and syrupy. I have an eerie feeling.

"You don't mean..."

"Don't I?"

"Well, do you?"

At that moment the door drifts open as if expecting a ghost. For a second nothing happens, and then in runs the goat bleating urgently. SM is looking at me. She puts her finger to her lips.

The light in the air shines like a thick green liquid.

34

All at once I'm back to my exact height. Like slipping into such a perfect fit it's my first sense of freedom. This height is me.

Hard to say how the image of him appears – a kind of bluish fiery still light, as if he is in the light, as if he's one slant on the light, like an image in a kid's hologram – you can't see it, but then you tip the grain of the light and there he comes walking like whatsisname in the fiery furnace.

Something shifts in my head, a trickle of shale, a small cliff-crumble on a windless day. I'm filling up with the wonder of it. All these years I've lived cut off from my own dead father, only because I've been looking askew – I've been choosing the wrong angle in the hologram.

Know what? It's like I've been missing a whole set of balls.

35

I can hear the sari begin to whisper, the rancid, buttery breathing, the brown slurp of fat bare feet. Fear is under a blanket. But I notice there's a nugget of confidence, about the size of a walnut. I can – I can push me up from face down. Urr – I can pack quite a snarl. I can almost turn me right over... I can.

As I turn, the sunlight is warm on my face. I've made it onto my back and am pushing out my bald tummy to display a kind of packed rotund confidence. There's a blaze of warmth that makes me crow and dribble. I can see them bent over me, the pair of them lit right through, even though they're against the light. I feel unzipped, so wide open I gasp, and am sliding back into the sweetness of it. I am, I'm falling asleep.

SM says: "So where's the threat?"

"No threat."

The green eyes go after me. One eyebrow's up. She's smiling.

"Who's at the back of it?"

"The back of what?"

"Everything."

"I don't know."

"Yes, you do."

"I don't."

"Come on."

"I do not know."

"Ayah?"

"Ah, Ayah, Ayah, AYAH."

36

I say: "That's where we came in." I'm having a cup of Red Zinger before I go.

"That's how you know when to stop." She's on tiptoe, reaching the jars of chutney up onto the top shelf.

"I feel grand," I say. I realize I'm hoping she's going to congratulate me.

"I feel I've come to the end of something. I feel it's the holidays. I feel like I've broken-up."

Sometimes she will take things too seriously – for instance she now says: "Begun to break up."

She's misunderstood, but I'm not prepared to labour it. Besides she's back with her notepad. I'm meanwhile thinking: Can't wait to tell Fiona, she'll be amazed. I feel such a sudden rush of warmth for her it's like a headlamp being shone in my eyes. I have to shut them against the glare.

SM says, like a doctor making an aside as she writes out a prescription: "When the cupboard door opened and the light came in you shot it. Right?"

"Hang on."

She smiles at that. I couldn't say where but she does smile, in fact I'd say she's close to laughing out loud. I'm right.

She says: "Sorry, I'm trying not to crease myself. Where were we? Oh yes, hang on, hang on, hang on... oops! See, you weren't man enough to stay with it – so you shot it. Which allowed you to feel you'd shot him too."

I say: "Come along, let's be serious."

"Didn't you say he was shot in the war?"

I'm getting used to this sort of nonsense.

"He was. But I never said it."

"Oh," she said innocently. "I thought you did. I thought you said he'd done the decent thing, something you'd have been scared shitless even to think of doing. And that he'd done it for you."

I think: Shit! Shit! Shit! Silently. At the top of my voice.

She hands me the note.

We arrive from one direction and think we've arrived. But as long as we think we've arrived we're just passing through – which means we now need to come at it from the other direction, right? When one really does arrive one doesn't even notice – that's because it's like one's just blown in from every direction at once.

I admit I read it rather cursorily. I say: "Thanks," and hand it back for her to put in the Rayburn. I can't help feeling impatient. She seems determined not to concede I've achieved anything. Why, I suddenly feel more like my old self. Probably she's a bit jealous, and needs to suppose she holds all the tricks. I think: That's understandable. Women, especially these days, tend to feel inferior in some areas.

I say: "You know, you're looking tired."

Actually it's true. I feel concerned about her, in fact quite fatherly.

I say: "You're taking on much too much on your own with all this... I wave my hand in a manly way that will reduce the goat, the ducklings, the hotch-potch, the chutney and all the rest of it to manageable commonsense.

She says, "If you want it back, you only have to shout."

"I beg your pardon?"

"You've just offloaded it onto me. Your tiredness. But if you're so attached to it you can have it back. You might not know what to do with yourself when you get home if you're not wanked-out."

I feel irritated. This sort of fashionable women's talk – there's no arguing with it. They seem to think if they can be coarse enough they'll be as liberated as... well, as we men. I control myself though. I say: "Thank you, I do I feel completely different."

"Not completely. Completely would mean complete. You are of course, but you don't yet know it. Not completely."

I think: Christ! But say nothing.

As she follows me to the door there seem to be hundreds of animals fussing around her. Outside the evening is lighter by a couple of shades. The shadows are blue. There's a blackbird singing.

What in this twilight looks like someone having difficulty with a deckchair is the wolfhound getting to his feet. On his way indoors he stops to give my shirt a distasteful sniff. I think he's deciding that on balance, I'm not worth pissing on.

She says: "And when you're ready, which probably means when you're next in a panic, we can if you like work some more. Up to you."

I don't know why but I have this sudden impulse to flirt with her. I say: "We'll have to see what Ayah thinks about that. Personally, I don't see it'll be necessary. And besides, panics? I wouldn't know one if I met it in a darkened room."

She doesn't answer, just looks at me. In the green light her eyes are so still it's eerie. The green disembodied by the green. And yet concentrated into so much of a still presence I have the feeling I'm experiencing her as the aftershock of a great ringing sound.

"For you," she says, and hands me a jar of chutney. "For you and your wife. A chance to share the process."

"The process?"

She shrugs her shoulders. "Okay, lets just call it green tomato chutney."

37

I'm hurrying up the shadowy lane when the magpie pops up. The same thing, twig to twig – only this time he's silent. Something startles him – he flies off.

I have this uncanny feeling there's someone watching me, maybe over the hedge. I stop and look round. I think: This distinct sound of breathing, presumably it's me. Me or maybe it's the breathing.

Distinct, as if the breath were from over my shoulder, comes this stale waft of buttery cardamom.

38

Driving home I'm aware that a mist's coming down. I draw up by the steps but don't immediately get out of the car. I feel flat. In fact I feel exhausted. I'm trying to remember what all the excitement was about. I wind down the window. The garden's almost dark, and it's empty, as if summer had just moved out. Everything moody and silent – except for some inexplicable stirring of the Michaelmas daises.

The front door is open. Through in the kitchen there's a light, otherwise the house is dark. A damp neglected feel – as if the mist has come to stay. I hesitate – then do something idiotic. I knock.

The light goes out in the kitchen.

Wait... I think I heard the back door. I run on tiptoe. There is, there's someone leaving by the back way, the old track that leads round to the lane.

"Hey!" I shout, but the evening doesn't hear. Maybe I didn't actually call or maybe...

Whoever it is has now gone.

As I turn I take a breath of the mist. There's a muddy taste to it, like a flooded stream, and a kind of a new-skinned pelty stink. Dennis.

I stand there with my face twitching. So tired I can hardly move.

39

The kitchen is cold. A mouse playing scrabble in the cupboard where Fiona keeps her pulses. I'm looking for a note that might tell me – well, tell me about my supper for God's sake. Of course – it'll be in the oven. Before I reach the oven my face can feel the cold of it.

I'm running through the house calling – Fiona! Annabel!

I think: See, she's out. These days she seems always to be out.

The bedrooms are empty and cold. There's a dank animal sullenness everywhere, a used feeling.

As for the bathroom... I just don't believe it, the monstrosity in the mirror – young, open, a washed, shining clarity like someone who's seen the light after a good cry. There's a boy's brave face on it but, underneath, the pain is writhing like something in a sack. And, the final straw... a definite look of Dennis about the nose.

I think: Things aren't going at all well. Does that young woman know what she's doing. She's playing with fire. I think I'm going to have to... think I'll just give her a buzz. Well I am, I'm in a bit of a panic.

Wait... the phone's ringing.

I think: Caruso! What a time to ring.

40

Corny. In trouble. He's sobbing, or at any rate breathing with great difficulty.

I think: Poor devil, I suppose he's been duped by Caruso. At the same time he's speaking at top speed. Which is what he was doing when I picked up the phone.

"Hold everything," I say. Then shout: "Will you kindly stop. Take a deep breath. Start again at the beginning."

But he's too disturbed. Just keeps spilling it out. I'm beginning to wonder whether it's me he's speaking to. Maybe the wires are crossed. I have an inspiration.

"Corny," I yell. "Let the breathing handle the breathing." But he carries on. I just listen. His voice isn't natural, sounds as if he's down a well. Or shut in a cupboard.

He's saying: "...I'm working, boiling a new gesso, and all the time I'm thinking gold. Maybe I'm getting too excited. I hear this voice which could be my voice saying, 'Then the rivers disappeared in dry land.' I'm thinking about this and thinking gold, when I hear a voice. 'The King is thirsty.' I look up. There's an old tramp staggering in the doorway, holding out his tin. He's on his last legs. I run to fetch him a drink. There's nothing in the tap."

He seems to be getting increasingly agitated.

"Cornelius," I shout, "take it easy!"

He takes not a blind bit of notice – just goes echoing on.

"The old chap had sat down on the step. I think the peacock yelling had unsettled him. I thought he was having a seizure. He wasn't, he was laughing. Trying to get his breath and then laughing again. 'You don't get water that way dear,' he managed. 'This'ns the way you get water.' He held out his hand and clenched his fist. He clenched it so hard that the veins stood up in his temples and out of his neck and blue on the back of his hand. He gritted his teeth and clenched harder. Then with a grunt he let his hand go and his fingers unfold. I heard the water beginning to pour out of the tap. I ran for a glass. When I reached the old chap he was on his side. That's what he'd done, he'd died."

He sounds so agitated, breathing in wheezing sobs, I feel worried. I shout: "Come on now Corny, do yourself a favour." There's a click, and then the burr of the dialling tone.

I think: That was a damn fool thing to say.

I try to ring back – no reply.

I try again. This time when I pick up the phone there's a whole crowd of people. It sounds like a cosmic switchboard – every tongue imaginable. And there in the dimmest distances an operator speaking a reedy pigeon-English. It's Manila. She's putting somebody through. It's Caruso.

Caruso! I say: "Now just you listen to me, Caruso..."

At which point there's a click. Again, I'm left holding the dialling tone.

41

I go back to the kitchen. I need a cup of lemon-balm or something. Something for the nerves. This should do it, it's called Good Night.

Beside the kettle there's a note.

So where were you this afternoon? If you've been on the booze or something you can jolly well sleep on the sofa. Me and mum's been worried. A.

I think: Sleep on the sofa! How can they do this to me? Then I think: Ah, it's not so bad, at least they've been worried.

Then I think: Anyway, it's not me who's out now, it's her. Where the hell's she been? Eh?

While the sachet is brewing I think maybe I should get the Rayburn relit. I fetch sticks, firelighters. When I open it, it's alight, hot, stoked for the night. I don't know what to think.

I feel I can hardly climb the stairs I'm so tired.

Fiona's asleep on my side of the bed. I feel a terrible surge of emotion. I feel I would like to get at her with my hands, but whether to give a hug or to throttle her isn't entirely clear.

"Mum..." I say. And then I hear me snarl a couple of times like a black panther... in a thicket.

When I start to undress, I find I'm still clinging to the jar of chutney. Green Tomato.

3

BLACK

(blacker than black)

42

I've woken in a real mess. I'm no better. Actually I'm measurably worse. I can't decide whether to ask Fiona for a hug or not. It's a big decision. But it's pretty imperative I know what's what. If Fiona were mad at me for waking her – that could prove a lot. I'm not sure I'd be able to handle that. On the other hand I'm not sure I've any alternative.

I'm about to turn over in the dark and feel for her when I'm remembering this dream.

43

Another Exam Dream. The week-end before my Finals. I've left it late in the past but never this late. I've still not looked at Ancient History. There's no way I'm going to make it now. Suddenly, slap in the middle of the dream, I think: Mummy – must have a word with her, she's the one who could help.

I dash out into the quad. I pass Brian Telfont and a couple of his ghoulish heavies. They're dragging this freshman, a limp aesthete called Starkie, to toss him into the Fellows' fishpond. Starkie's pride is his hennaed beard. They have shaved one side of it off. I could interfere, but convince myself that I really must find mother.

I run up a staircase and down a corridor. I stop outside a door, number 110 – that's it. I go in, and guess what – here's who I've been looking for, but it's not mum, it's a young, rather beautiful, very impressive and commanding black woman. It is, it can only be Ayah. She's with several other people. I think: So what, I don't care anymore.

I start to tell her my problem with the imminence of the exam and my shameful failure to get down to the Ancient History. As I speak, I feel: Yes, but even now I could still do it.

I say: "I know what to do but I want to know what you have to say."

She takes me by the arm and says: "Before any discussion there's something you need to accept."

She leads me to the sofa. There, her face surly, eyes very much grey, deliberately distant, is Fiona.

Ayah says: "Your wife has always rejected your brother's advances, but in the last two days has felt like accepting them."

It strikes me that this is somehow a comment on my weakness, and is linked to my defeatist attitude towards the exam.

No wonder I've woken in a mess.

44

I think: That's it. It's going to have to be a hug. I put out my hand and at the same time whisper urgently: "Fiona!"

She's not there.

I put on the light. She isn't there. In fact it doesn't look as if the bed's been slept in.

I think, calmly: Okay, so this is where I discover what happens when one has a major crack-up. Then I think: Pills – I'll take some pills. Where would one find pills this time of night? I remember someone who stayed, a neurotic – and by neurotic I mean genuinely neurotic – school-friend of Fiona's. She left behind a bottle of corkers. Blue ones. They're in the bathroom cupboard.

My hand's shaking so much I practically knock my teeth out on the tumbler. I look up. There he is in the mirror, gulping down the pills. What a spectacle! What a wimp! Christ!

I put the pill bottle in the cupboard and tiptoe back to bed.

45

I'm woken by a bang, as if the front door's been snatched shut by a gust of wind. Stilettos in the downstairs passage. The kitchen door. And then, I'm virtually sure, laughter. Fiona and Jennie most likely. I'm not absolutely sure about the laughter but one thing is certain: If it was laughter it's me they were laughing at.

It's after ten. Outside there's boisterous sunlight and a tearaway wind, gust after gust chasing it's tail, knocking down the *aster novae-angliae*. Where I've reached is the point where one may as well stop in bed for all the difference it's going to make to anybody. I mean no one's even brought me a cup of tea. It is, it's pathetic.

Ten be blowed, it's after eleven. I think: Jennie's been here half the morning with nothing to do. Which someone who's lost touch with his commodities can ill-afford. That gets me out of bed.

46

No sign of Jennie. I think: Maybe she's walked out. Maybe she never came. But someone's laid the mail out neat on my desk. I see at a glance there's nothing from Penang. Anything on the answerphone? Yes, from Frank, the head of my assembly team. They've finished the job: conservatory up, the house is empty, not a dickey-bird from you know who, they want their money, everything's ready for the gold leaf merchant.

As I switch back the machine I hear laughter from the kitchen. I think: Okay, so this is where I confront the pair of them. Nothing wimpish about the way I set my jaw. I don't bother to knock before bursting in.

Empty. Everything spick and span, the Rayburn purring... I think: I need a cup of tea, a real brown rouser, which reminds me, I must introduce Fiona to Red Zinger – she'll love Red Zinger.

47

The kettle's taking forever to boil. I think: That Cornelius was in a devil of a stew last night. I wonder if I should check he's alright. Actually I need to ring him to tell him he can start work up at Caruso's place. Or maybe I should tell him not to start work up at Caruso's. Not till I hear something definite about my commodities.

I dash into the sitting-room and dial the number. Corny answers.

"Yes?" he sounds offhand and impatient.

"It's me. I rang to say not to..."

"Yes?" he says again much as to say, come on, get on with it – this remember's the chap who last night was involving me in his own self-inflicted blitzkreig. But then he says: "Hang on."

I can hear some other person in the background talking. The pair of them laugh in a snide, raucous way. Then nothing. Corny's put his hand over the mouthpiece. I can tell. I think: They're saying something about me. Now he's taken his hand away.

The other person is still talking but I can't hear... wait, yes I can. I don't believe this. I can't hear precisely what he's saying but I can hear the tone. It's not a tone I'm likely to mistake. Caruso.

I see, this means the pair of them are in cahoots. Probably 'doing themselves a favour lad' – at my expense. There's a pause. Again I hear them laugh. And then Corny comes back on air. He's cupped the mouthpiece with his hand and is whispering in an intimate way: "You may of course think antimony's bluish-white and brittle, but this sort is entirely different, it's black and loamy. The magical black earth Adam smuggled out of Eden. The black blacker than black. In it the gold has been sown like a grain of wheat."

A click. And then the damned dialling tone. He's clonked in my ear. I feel the air hum in an odd way, as if the phone is ringing but not making a sound. Like when one's been slapped in the face. I feel the welt coming up on my cheek.

I think: I think I'll ring him back and yell at him. And then I think: The hell with it. I feel like a kid who's feeling it would be good strategy to cry but who's in too much of a temper. My eyes smart, my face is thoroughly contorted – but I can't come up with the tears.

I go growling back down the passage to the kitchen.

I say: "What the hell are you doing here?"

48

I say: "I said what the hell are you doing here?"

"She said if she's not around to go on in and make myself at home."

"So you've decided to move in."

It's Dennis. He's sitting, drinking a cup of tea. Out of my cup. I have this special cup. The big one.

I say: "And who's she?"

"She's, you know, Fiona."

"That's right. I do know Fiona. My wife."

He says: "She said she'd like to see my bags."

"She did, did she?"

"I make these saddlebags. They're handbags, but I make them on the lines of saddlebags. Like this one."

Something different about Dennis today. More flesh to him and somehow sleek. A sheen – as if someone's been feeding him up. I find this very unsettling. I bet it's deliberate, a kind of bravado prior to the showdown. I try leaning to one side so I can get a good look at him in profile. That's it, the presentable bit around the nose, the bit that presumably looks like me, its more pronounced. For some reason he becomes increasingly shifty.

When I've had a good look at him I say: "What was that you were saying?"

"Handbags – like this one."

I say: "Looks more like a saddlebag. Anyway I'm afraid you've missed her. She's not at home."

At precisely this moment, from up in the bathroom or the landing or wherever, comes the clearest most contented: "Kiss me in the rain, make me feel I'm a child again..."

Dennis and I are looking at each other. I suspect he's playing safe by imitating my expression. Suddenly he's become illuminated by a cocky glow, and there's nothing he can do to disguise the fact.

I say: "Yes, Annabel's never at home this time of day. She goes to college first thing. I'm making myself a cup of tea. My secretary's on holiday. What about you?"

He says: "Me? I don't... no, I don't have a secretary."

"You don't? Oh well, what about a good brown rouser?"

Christ! That's the last thing he needs!

"I beg your pardon?"

"A nice cup of tea?"

"Yep, ta, I do – I have a cup of. Already, already. Someone's at the door."

I look down the passage. Jennie. What's she been up to – washed with a bar of jokeshop soap? Black smudges all over her face.

I say: "That'll be my secretary. She's just back from holiday. That's why she's late. By the way that's my cup."

I go to the front door. Jennie's face is flooded. Her black eye-liner's spreading through it like an oil-slick. For some reason I feel quite ashamed of her.

I say: "What's up for God's sake?"

"I knew you didn't want me-e-e back."

"Ssh!" I hiss. I don't want Dennis picking up on this. Nor Fiona. Fiona's stopped singing by the way – whatever that may mean. She's probably upstairs listening.

I say: "Don't be daft. You know as well as I do I think you're..." I pause and then raise my voice. "...Fiona and I think you're indispensable." Then I hiss: "Come to that, why're you so goddam late?"

"You said, you said, you said..."

"Ssh"

"...you'd come for me."

I'm having an idea, though at this stage it's still rather vague. I say: "Come on in, you need a good strong cup of tea. There's someone I want you to meet." I'm having another idea. I push past Jennie into the kitchen. I say to Dennis: "Did you, er, read that note?"

"Yes. Thank you."

I say: "Well it was none of your damn business."

His eyes go little and his lower lip flops.

"Had my name on it."

"Not that note – Annabel's note."

"Really – did Annabel leave me a note?" It's pathetic.

"No, she left *me* a note. We have little jokes. Very private. Ha, ha, ha. This is my secretary, Jennie. You two should get to know each other. Bags in common."

Dennis says: "Hullo. You into bags too?"

Jennie is dabbing her face here and there with a tissue. She gives Dennis a tearful weaselly look, as if she's heard this bags line before.

Dennis tries again: "Had a nice holiday?"

Jennie gives a convulsive 'after-the-crack-up' sniff and then manages breathlessly: "Yes thank you, only I haven't taken my holidays yet."

I say: "I'm going to leave you two young things together. Got work to do. Dennis, you make Jennie a cup of tea. A good strong one."

But already I'm thinking: Nope can't leave these two together. Fatal. So I sit down at the table beside Jennie.

I say: "And Dennis you can make me one too." But what I'm thinking is: Did I? Did I leave Annabel's note by the kettle? I jump up.

"No, you sit down. I'm going to make 'em." I push past Dennis. Annabel's note's gone. That's it, I've got it in my pocket. I say: "There, I've put on the kettle. Dennis, you make the tea. Now if you'll excuse me I've work to do."

I know it's risky leaving the pair of them together but – Oh the hell with it.

49

The Heron. An extraordinary thing happens. I decide against the study. Instead I slip out the back way.

I think: I think I'll string some onions.

The onions are drying in the open shed at the end of the lawn. I can't be seen from the house.

The day has become more unsettled: one moment it's mellow

fruitfulness and tortoiseshells on the *sedum spectabile;* the next the sun's gone, the wind's turned grey and started whimpering in the telephone wires. I can see I'm agitated from the way I fumble the strings. But I can't keep my mind even on that – I've begun to think about the heron.

The day Fiona and I moved in, nearly two years ago, we saw this huge lanky bird fly over the house, heading for the stream.

I said: "Look, it's a pelican or something."

"It's a stork."

"I sincerely hope not!"

"Well any way it's our lucky bird."

We've allowed the idea to grow that the heron will fly by every year and that when we see it we'll know everything's fine.

I'm thinking: Know what? We haven't seen the heron this year. That's a clincher, that has to be really unlucky

I look up. Beyond the lawn, standing some thirty yards away in the drive is a tall, grey-looking man. My immediate reaction is: This man isn't what he seems. He looks unfamiliar, but I feel I've seen him before. He's staring up at the house in an ominous way like that character in Hardy's novels who keeps returning after forty years with a lot on his mind.

I continue stringing onions determinedly but I'm watching him out of the corner of my eye. He's certainly holding something in his arms: it's grey like himself and he holds it kind of cradled.

I hear the front door open. There's Fiona on the steps in her blue cashmere jumper, looking young and stunning. The man is talking to her – about what he has in his arms.

Christ, it's our heron.

His voice is crackly but I can hear him say he's found it in trouble beside the stream. He's not sure if it's stunned or faint from hunger. Or if it's dead. It does seem to be warm. Fiona runs back into the house. Single-mindedly I continue stringing my Sturons – well, perhaps not single-minded.

Here's Fiona again, down the steps, running to the man. She says something to him. He shifts the body of the bird into the crook of one arm, and with the hand of that arm is holding its neck. With the other hand, the fingers, he forces open the beak. Fiona, calm as a theatre-sister, is pouring something down its throat from a white plastic spoon. I know what that'll be, the miraculous arnica. Little white pills – Annabel's boyfriend gave them her last winter. He thought she might need it to help with the shock of him walking out. She didn't – but nowadays the least bruise or jolt or life-crisis and we slip one under the tongue. I could use a couple now – high-potency.

I'm watching now. I can't grasp all of what's hitting me except it's like a battery of light – my love for this sure, joyful woman in her blue jumper. It makes me feel distinctly unsound. With everything in the balance, still she is deft and methodical as she works on the fateful bird.

To give it the medicine she's had to dilute the pill in a teaspoon of water. My eyes are pricking with tense tears. It feels as if at the same time I'm shouting and holding my breath. I feel cut off. I see everything in the clearest detail, but I'm cut off from it.

What's happening? The man seems to be having trouble holding the bird. The thing's come alive. It's struggling in his arms. Fiona leans forward to settle the heron with her hand. It draws back from her, is poised a moment quite like a snake. Then it stabs.

Fiona has taken a step back. She has both hands over her eyes. The man shields his head as the heron struggles free. With slow lurching flaps it is gaining height. I hear it thinly, the one searing, gloating shout, and then the bird-tatters are caught by a gust and toppled over the trees. Blood is leaking from between Fiona's fingers.

Whatever it is it's on my back and I can't break away. The grip of it, that's the problem – it has the muscle of undentable anger. I need to run to Fiona. Besides she's all in the world I want. But I can't. The more I force myself the tighter the grip. I feel the anger taking over, moving through me with its terrible cold.

The man has gone. Fiona walks slowly up the steps. She looks down at her fingers at the blood, and then touches her forehead. The wound is low down, almost exactly between her eyes. Right where she carries that little questioning frown.

Again I try to shout. I feel I've never been hurt by anything so much as this inability to move. Or rather to move as I would like. Because I can still move – I'm quite able to continue stringing these infernal onions.

50

Still stringing the onions.

Dennis hasn't left.

What bearing does that have? A whole lot of bearing. All I want is to go in and tell Fiona I love her, and that the worst thing ever to happen to me was not being able to break from the anger and run to her when she was skewered by the heron. Why don't I do just that? Because Dennis is in there probably tending her bloody wound! Or else he's discussing bags. And there isn't a goddam law to protect me. All I can do is stand here, twitching, and stringing my onions.

The front door has opened. There's Dennis on the steps. He stops and looks back over his shoulder. Presumably Fiona's in the doorway, waving him goodbye. I can't see Fiona, but I can see Dennis. He's carrying his leatherworks, and over his arm he's carrying something else.

"Bye then." The tone is unctuous. As an afterthought he gives whatever's over his arm a wave. Whatever be blowed – they're my old trousers. In the immediate shock, in my utter, inexpressible torment of betrayal, I drop my champion Giant Sturons on the cobbled floor.

"And thanks for the trousers. They'll be handy for work."

Handy for work! Those are my special trousers. I've had them donkey's years. Everything's suddenly clear – I should have seen this coming. Fiona's been looking for an excuse to get rid of those trousers of mine ever since, well even before we were married. And she chooses today. I just don't believe it. Trousers, the symbol of, of, of... She's given them to Dennis. That's it. Now there's going to have to be a scene.

"Old bags for new!" That's Dennis being impish in the drive.

I lay my string of onions in a deckchair. As I turn to stride after him I do what the Duke of Edinburgh does, give my nose a businesslike rub with my left hand.

My whole world blurs.

I don't know how long I stand there staring at the clenching and unclenching fingers of my left hand and by sheer force of will holding down the resounding, imminent dark. It's coming for me again. This time from under the lawn. It's very near the surface. Very near. In fact the surface is beginning to crack-up.

I run across the lawn and get in the car. I can't say whether the tears are grief or fury, but they don't make driving any easier. Any more than does my repeatedly taking my left hand off the wheel to check finger by finger that what I'm not prepared to think could have happened, really has happened.

It has.

Where am I heading? The way I'm feeling, I'd be the last person to know.

Except, I could use a nice cup of Red Zinger, a real red rouser. So... let the driving do the driving. No way I can cope with this on my own. I was out of my depth in any case, even before being hexed by the heron, terminally hexed. What else, at this precise loaded moment, with him walking out of my house with my trousers, given by my wife, would account for the uncanny disappearance of, of, of... my wedding-ring?

51

No animals around. The door open, creaking a little in the drab breeze. I'm thinking: She's moved out. That's torn it. What a generation, can't stick to anything... when I hear inside somebody grunt, and then a piece of furniture shift.

I yell: "Alright if I come in?"

Silence. I don't remember this smell... like a tannery on a hot day. Then she's there in the doorway. No... Christ! Yes, it is, it's her.

She looks wicked. Her hands dripping blood. There's blood on her...

Laura Ashley be damned. She's wearing some sort of khaki cross between a boiler-suit and a combat-jacket. Her features are translucent lead – dull and vivid. In the green electrical eyes the glint is wicked. I think: She's just murdered someone. I've walked right in on it.

"What you want? You have an appointment? No, of course you bloody don't. Well I'm busy, so bugger off!"

She wipes her nose on the back of her wrist, which fetches a clotted red smear across her left cheek.

I say: "Something's cropped up." Which if she's in this sort of mood I reckon is safer than trying to explain. Some of the finer details, my old trousers for example, might seem a bit limp. Not the ring though. That spells heartbreak in anyone's book.

"I've lost my ring. My wedding ring."

I can't help my voice cracking a little.

"So what have you lost? Your ring! Oh dear, that's a bit of a bugger!" Her laughter is lethal, and she fixes me with an amber-gone-tigerish glare. I feel my mouth opening and shutting, but I don't think I'm managing to say anything.

She says: "Go on, you better clear off." The voice is steel, as if she's had the strop to it.

I don't move. Something in me's begun to tick. I watch her wipe her red sticky hands, the front then the back, on her apron. I seem to be growing calm.

I say: "How do you mean?"

"Clear off. Before you get scratched. This place is foul with shit. Breathe and someone with your sagging testosterone count would be straight down with tetanus."

I'm calm enough to ignore this. I say: "What, I mean what are you up to?"

She looks me over as if thinking she would rather be a man short than pick me for her team before she says: "You're prepared are you, to get your hands shitty?"

I feel myself nod. She turns, signals with her head I'm to follow her into the cottage. She's saying: "You're a wanker. No sooner get home than you start popping pills, right?"

I don't answer.

She says: "We have a cure for wankers."

That's when I catch sight of... the table. There's a corpse on it. The legs already skinned.

53

Consumerism. The room smells rancid, mutton-sweet. She hands me a blood-sticky knife.

"You take off the feet. There, through the bottom joint. You like my dream? It's unreal, right? You better believe it. This one isn't ancient history."

"How, how did you know?"

"Like, what?"

"Ancient History! My dream. I always flunk on Ancient History. I mean it's another weird coincidence."

She sneers. "So he flunked his Ancient History. Okay, then lets revise a spot of Ancient History. Shit, no wonder you choose to live double-glazed in a conservatory."

She's working a flap of skin that'll lift between the sheep's back legs. In she thrusts with her right fist, punching the skin free from the meat. I'm struggling with the knife, trying at the same time to get a grip on the slithery little hooves. By rights I should be retching – but I keep going back to this solid thing forming in my stomach.

She says: "Right let's get 'im up."

On tiptoe she can thread the rope through an iron eye on the main beam. Tied to the other end of the rope's a hook. Somehow she spikes both the ankles, and I help her haul the carcass up.

She says: "Where's your knife? Right. Now slit him, just the skin, down his tummy top to bottom. Okay, now get your hands in there. That's it."

I feel the solid thing in me clearer than ever. I'm getting the hang of being in touch with it. It's a very definite anger. It feels grand, in fact it's a pretty exuberant, gratifying physical feeling.

She's saying: "Last time, there was a moment I thought you might make it. I was wrong, the rot's too deep. The consumer virus, you're riddled with it. I didn't think a centre could be so rotten."

I want to laugh. She doesn't know about this solid thing forming in my stomach. At the moment it's tough-going, punching the skin free from the rump.

I'm thinking: In my book a consumer's no bad thing – provided he pays his bills. Which is of course a reference to Caruso. And a sharp reminder that when I next have a suitable moment I must examine how, in the light of that last weird phone-call, Corny fits into this commodities business. Too neatly by half if...

She's cut the skin from around the anus and tail. We get a grip and pull together. I don't believe it. The entire skin gathers up to the brisket as if we're helping the sheep out of a tight sweater.

She says: "Here, take the knife. Now it's the head. Not there, next vertebrae, right next to the skull. Go for it!"

In the centre I'm hard. Watch out, Caruso! The whole business is slimy-cold, the knife slews in my grip. I'm making a hell of a mess but I'm getting there.

I say: "So what you were just saying is, consumerism's a sort of virus."

My expression is quite hard, right to the point.

SM says: "It's the wanker's way of looking. Doesn't matter what it is, watching footie on the box, watching Eastenders, reading yoga books, watching a bit of bum in the street, if one's a consumer like you one's spending, wanking, running yourself down. Black hole syndrome. Good, you made it. Gimme the knife."

"Okay, so what does one do?" I detect a definite edge to my voice. "I mean what's opposite to consuming?"

"Like, it's another way of looking at a thing. You just look at it, whatever it is, creatively and you've made it. That way you're working on yourself. You're making gold."

I think: See, now she's into gold. Just what I suspected, the Caruso-Cornelius connection! So I wink and say: "Ah, you mean commodities."

"I mean..." She looks at me chillingly. "Hand me that cleaver!"

"Er..." I say, "What shall I do with this?" For some time I've been holding the head by one ear and trying to look creatively into a sheepish dead eye.

"There on the table, and then fetch those buckets. Listen!"

From out in a shed comes a great warbling moan.

"See – creative! Doesn't miss a trick. He gets the head. Okay, hold this."

This is a couple of inches of rectum. She's snipped round the anus and pulled the thing out. Christ. Still if it is the way to show I can act creative I'll hold it in my teeth.

I say: "A step up from Eastenders, eh?"

She looks violence at me. "Know what's worse than a wanker? A wanker who thinks he's cut above... when actually he's cut below."

She ties a piece of string round the bit of rectum I'm holding. She says: "Let go," and hands me back the knife.

"Right," she says pointing to the inner belly sack. "Top to bottom. Careful mind. Put your finger over the point of the blade. If you puncture the gut we'll be in a shitty mess."

Now we work in silence. The hard solid rage is through me so strong I have to work to not let the pleasure of it growl. She hauls down the rectum and bowel. I hold them while she unfastens the cold swilly bladder and tugs the liver away from the backbone. The load of it comes shimmering away into a bucket.

She says: "Fancy some tripe?" And is pulling the gut through her hands as if looking for a patch on an inner tube.

I grin but don't speak. I feel I'd not be responsible for what I might say.

She says: "Pass me the hacksaw. You asked the question, here's your answer. Consumer's a wanker who lives a cosy double-glazed existence in his pre-pack conservatory and doesn't know that when his... correction, when your wedding ring's gone missing it's time you killed your own fucking wife. Right?"

I think: Steady on! Then I shrug. To be honest I'd forgotten about all that.

I say: "I'm not altogether sure what you mean."

"Mean? I'll show you what I mean. 'Bye bye sweetheart.'"

And she starts to saw the carcass in half – down the length of the backbone.

She says: "Okay, now fetch the mattress."

53

SM says: "Christsake! let the breathing do the breathing."

I say: "Anyway what makes you so sure I'm a consumer or... or a wanker or whatever damn thing you call it?"

She wipes the blood off her hands, the palms then the backs of them, on her khaki-pocketed combat gear.

She says: "Because last time when you were leaving you toyed, yes toyed with the idea of making a pass at me. Only a right wanker would..."

"GRRRRRRR." That's the devil. He's leapt out at me from behind a bush. A real slippery blue-black demon. Grinning. Gives me a hell of a shock.

54

Now it's me who's beginning to laugh. The devil's a regular devil. We grapple with each other on the mattress, wrestling with a deal of huffing and puffing. I'm catching up on some laughing, a kind of green, rude, ruddy laughter. I punch him playfully.

I say: "You devil, you."

And so he is. A blue-black, sleek young shining demon. About my size and full of mischief. He and I are good mates. He stands there shock staring naked, sinewy and generally bristling, grinning warmly and wickedly. He couldn't be more pleased with his prank – on my back all these years, scaring me to death, pretending to be some inconceivably unconfrontable devilish big deal. But now we're real good mates and together we can scare the shit out of anybody.

55

SM says: "You've got a nerve twitching in your jaw. Go into that."

Sometimes she drives me mad. This blue-black fellow and I are just getting into a conversation about Fiona. We're so to speak going over her bit by bit – and are agreeing she's a good thing. Really good conversation. Plenty of tongue-clicking and the occasional randy whoop.

She says: "Go on, go into it."

I'm wondering, why should my teeth be clenched? Why, when at last I'm really beginning to enjoy myself, when I've at last got together with this blue-black chap – why should there be something else to go into? This wondering seems to make my teeth clench even tighter. Suddenly forcing its way past the teeth comes an extraordinary wailing noise. Know what I think this is?

I say: "I suppose you're too young to remember what this is?"

She's got an old hatchet in her hand, is getting the chops undone.

She says; "Sounds like it's the air-raid siren. Take cover, here comes Ancient History!"

56

The planes are coming in again, straight up the estuary. I'm running up and down the beach but where the hell is she?

Mummy!

Tut-tut-tut-tut. The bullets puff the sand in sort of jumping strings.

Mummy! Yes, so this time it's this time and where the bloody hell is she this time?

Know what? I'm the one who's made to feel ashamed – for kicking up such a fuss. She, on the other hand has gone AWOL, abandoned me. And she gets off scot-free.

What does she say? She says: "Your father's away fighting in the war, and you make that sort of hullaballo! I'm ashamed of you."

I'm thinking: In a minute she is, she's going to tell everyone about the green knickers.

57

Fear's coming back. Damn-it. This time above and slightly behind. Cardamom flavour, stale ghee and definitely brown. I don't feel particularly daunted.

I say to my demon: "The two of us can handle this. Easy."

I turn and take a quick look at her and begin to growl.

I say to him: "Go on then, you get her." I feel the fear, and I feel we're stronger than the fear.

I face her – you know who it is? That hideous accusing aspect of hers and ooo... I can take it. I can, I can sop up any amount of this. I think maybe I'll laugh, but what's happening?

Instead of doing what I ought to be doing, ie: taking her by the throat and bashing her head against the wall until her brains spill, I'm beginning to go soft.

"Poor mum." Poor mum?

Poor mum, for Christsake!

I'm reaching up with one hand to touch her hair. Then with both hands to take hold of her head, to draw it down, to have her lay it on my chest. Odd – I'm in touch with her pain. I'm tapped into it. Poor love. Poor dear love. Poor love grown old, all alone – that loneliness year after year without him. Without dad. Because he got killed in the War.

Oh Christ!

58

SM says: "What're you playing at? You get your chance and then you cop out."

"Did I?" I say this serenely, from the standpoint of unencumbered love.

"You let them off the hook. You've not shifted a thing."

The solid whatever it is in my stomach gives a sudden twist and I growl. I think: You know, maybe she's right. But what do I do about it?

SM's trimming the scrag-end. She stops to sharpen the knife.

She says quietly: "Didn't you say she'd just leave you with an old woman while she went off with him dancing till dawn?"

"Christ, did I say that?"

"And that whenever you, like, raised the roof, she'd say: 'Hush, whatever would your father have said? He went and died for you, don't you forget it.'"

"Yes, I did yes." She's got this thing in my stomach beginning to thrash around.

"And that she'd leave that old woman to feed you and muck you out and because it wasn't what needed to happen, if you were to be a real little man she wasn't ever going to let you see, let alone get your mits on her tits?"

"MUMMA!" I yell. I think it's some sort of corroboration. "Did I, I mean did I really say that?"

"So your father was a soldier. I expect he was a Colonel or some damned thing. Ever thought you might have been something of a disappointment? He found you in the cupboard, didn't he? Oh dear, I don't suppose you remember what he found you were wearing?"

59

Women.

"... isn't that what women have always done? Wanted their sons to be brave soldier boys?"

Her voice is suddenly horrific – a knife so sharp that everything it touches falls apart without the least resistance.

I think: My guess is she's psychotic. I realise now, she's got some sort of problem. Probably with men. She shouldn't be loose with that knife. I wonder how she killed the sheep?

Also, I don't like the way it's getting so dark in here.

Maybe I should try to defuse things?

I say manfully: "Yes but you know women. I mean it hasn't been easy for women. Look at all this women's lib and..."

Defuse! The way her eyes have begun to spark it looks as if I've set the whole munitions dump alight. She is, she's going to take the knife to me.

She's seething: "Wouldn't it just take someone who's hocked his balls to buy that horseshit!" Suddenly her voice goes bitterly tired. "You can't see it, can you? The one who's frustrated and the one who's doing the frustrating they're two consenting experiences of the one fucking frustration."

I say: "I see."

Actually the only thing I see is her bending over me and waving her knife like she's a one woman peripatetic slaughter business.

She's off again, very quiet, as if reciting something from memory: "Daddies have little girls. Girls whose daddies were little boys, yes who were dressed in soldier suits by mummies who are still daddies' little girls who don't let their boys see their soft bodies because that would stop them growing into brave soldier boys. And who do they say's in charge of all this? Daddies of course, because they bring home the bread and fight the war and... shit. Do daddies sew the little soldier suits? First time the little boy opens his eyes he sees his mum's adoring smile – that's when he knows he's been cut for a soldier. Should he ever be tempted to forget it, she'll be there with her little white feather. 'Surely you're not making a fuss' she says, 'If daddy knew he'd a poufda for a son he'd turn in his grave.' See what she's achieved? Generation after generation of mum's boys in little soldier suits whose fathers turn in their graves because they know their sons will take after them, yes which means being up there in the dark in the spare-room cupboard humping themselves in their sister's knickers. Why green by the way?"

60

"I beg your pardon?"

"The knickers are obvious but why green?"

I don't know about that but I know there's something horrendous going on in my stomach. I snarl and writhe around. It does occur to me my problem could be rabies. I try to hold myself together with both hands.

I say: "Quick, what do I do?"

Actually it comes out pretty much as a rabid lupine whine. She whips round. The sneer stops my writhing in its tracks. She says: "I know what I'd do but you might not have enough man for it. You make up your own mind. What do you want to do?"

"I want, I want..."

"Shit! For a moment I thought you were ready to go for real."

"I am. Grrrr!"

"So what you want?"

"I wanna..."

"Yes?"

"Grrr... I want to fuck her."

What am I talking about! Someone's putting words in my mouth.

"You do, do you? No you don't. But you're getting warmer."

"I'm going to get... I'm going to have to kill her."

"Who?"

"Christsake! I don't know."

"Come on – who?"

"I don't... No, no, no..."

I think: I can't think how she gets to be here, walking through this shadowy boneshop, glowing like Ophelia's ghost, or how she gets to be so pastey-faced and prim and white-puddingy.

"Fiona," I whisper.

"Okay. So get on with it."

I try to say no, but this thing writhing in my stomach won't hear of it. SM's fetching something from the cupboard. A cushion. She tosses it to me.

She says: "Go on get on with it. Don't be such a wanker."

Whooosh! That's done it. I'm into it, roaring. Ker-rist. I'm sleek shiny-blue with demon strength. I do some clubbing, real haymakers, and some putting in the knees. Her neck's a hank that comes a yard long. I knead that till her eyes go yellow and snarl at me.

So I hadn't noticed – it's mum I'm throttling. My fingers are enjoying themselves, but this... hang on, now it's, it's this Ayah person, and she's proving a bit of a handful. I'm trying to throttle her but I don't seem able to get my hands round her throat. I don't seem to be having the same sort of success with Ayah.

61

A Dreadful Event. Ayah's getting on top of me. I feel strongly persuaded to tell her I'm sorry. But I glimpse my demon hugging himself and doubled up with wicked rude laughter – and so instead I manage: "Fucking women!"

The Ayah person rises to this. She takes over completely. I'm not sure that makes clear what I mean. I mean I'm actually experiencing all the astonishing tides of being Ayah. Ayah's possessed me. I am Ayah, and something quite hideous is beginning to happen.

That solid thing in my stomach is on the move.

First I register the movement in my head and chest, as if it is attached even here by strands – which are beginning to tear.

All the time I'm thinking I should shout, "I'm sorry." But what's happening's happening and there's nothing will stop it now. I feel a warm irrigation exploring my lower part, my sort of bowel or entrails or whatever it is down there. Something delicious about all this uncomfortable movement – until the racking starts and I realize the business is coming to a head.

Maybe it's at this point I know the way it's going. I feelingly know why I need Ayah. The clamping and unclamping in my stomach is coming faster. And faster.

SM says: "The breathing, let it do the breathing."

I feel myself nod to her, and as I do that I realize I'm on the move. Up off my back. I'm squatting there on the mattress with my hands on my knees.

It happens then. I reach down thinking maybe I'm involved in some mime. But my fingers – they've caught hold of it for real. And there from out of my... from down out of me I drag this writhing, wet, black thing. I don't know if it's a dream fragment but sure as hell I see it and can feel the black polished fish-slipperiness of its skin. About a foot long, pinheaded, a black wriggling shiny pitch-black imp-baby. Wriggling like fury. I've latched onto it. I can feel the high-voltage imp-power drilling my fingers. Violently I flick it off like it's dead, tacky afterbirth or something. Fling it so it smashes on the slate floor.

As if a switch had been switched the anger's gone from me. Anger I hadn't known was there but can feel now it's gone. I'm kneeling there intact. Christ, I'm drenched.

I think: I can't even think of moving for the time being I'm so bushed. But I'm clear and empty and full right up.

"Okay?" SM says gently.

I say: "Mummy. Ooops sorry. Know what? It was wriggling like fury."

Even though it's painful I begin to laugh.

I say: "Like fury. Get it?

62

A Girl Forming. I open my eyes. I've been into a thin little vision or dream, something momentary, like coloured breath on a mirror, like a filmy transfer on the surface of being almost asleep – and what was it I saw? A dust eddy caught up off the ground, being swirled into a spiral column and then becoming a shadowy form, the vestige of a girl being spun out of clay. I feel an intense excitement about the possibilities of this girl – but that's it.

I've opened my eyes because the phone's ringing.

63

The phone's by the door. As she goes to it SM wipes her blood-sticky hands on her thighs. She's picked up the receiver and without saying a word to it has put it down in the basket of Bramleys.

"It's for you," she says.

I think: Nobody knows where I am, so it has to be important. I pick up the phone and say cautiously: "Mr Caruso?"

Cornelius. He's out of breath, says he hasn't a great deal of time. I think: What the hell's he mean. He's not dying is he?

I say: "You alright?"

"Alexander found the tomb of Hermes..." He stops for breath. It flashes through my mind this could be code for Caruso in the underworld having got his hands on a batch of outlawed commodities.

I think: Christ! But what I do is hiss: "Yes, yes." Probably because he sounds so on edge, like someone on the run who suspects the phone's tapped.

"Just listen, I'll do the talking. 'And outside is a certain tree with glorious greenness inside. And on it there sat a stork, as it were calling itself the circle of the moon. And there he built golden seats and put a fitting end to his travels.'"

He's breathing elaborately – as if expecting appreciation.

I say: "That it? Look Corny I've had rather a weird day. But since you're on the phone there is this question..."

"Stork. Pelican. Heron. Same thing. Thought you'd want to know."

"You did?"

He gasps, irritable: "The philosophical vessel, the type of Christ. Now are you with it? He sticks your wife between the eyes. The meritorious wound. It signifies the opening of the Ajna chakra, the eye that sees without seeing. Blood signifies the coming to life, the resurrective wound. It's your wound. Get it?"

I'm getting this bad feeling. I say: "Hang on, have you been seeing Fiona or something?"

"What d'you mean? I was there wasn't I? I could see you skulking around in the shed."

Christ! "You mean that was you?"

"No it was Alexander the Great. Pull yourself together, you don't suppose you're going to get through this on your own? Now listen. You wanted to know about the green, didn't you? Green in general and green in particular."

I'm feverishly massaging my forehead. "Yes," I say, "I believe I did."

"Ssh, listen to this! 'But thou hast inquired concerning the greenness, deeming the bronze to be a leprous body on account of the greenness it hath upon it. Therefore I say unto thee that whatever is perfect in the bronze is that greenness only, because that greenness is straightway changed by our majesty into our most true gold.'"

I just catch the last word before his voice wavers away.

There's a click and then the dialling tone. I look at the receiver in a tired way and put it back on the hook.

SM's standing beside me. Suddenly she's quite small. I'm trying to be creative about this feeling I'm getting that I'd really love her to give me a hug. Or that'd I'd really love to pick her up and give her a hug. Even if she does stink of offal. She's holding something in her hands.

She says: "You alright?" Her voice is definitely gentle. I don't know if I can bear it.

I say: "Know who that was?"

"Ssh," she says. " I know. Hermes."

I shake my head, but she nods emphatically.

She says: "Messenger between conscious and unconscious worlds."

I say: "Corny says Hermes is dead."

She says: "Good. That's the best way to come alive. Why else would you want to kill your wife?"

I look at her. It's almost dark but I think I can see a secret softness in her eyes. I think: There's something very odd going on. Almost dark yet it's amazing how green her eyes are.

I say: "Oh yes, remember those green knickers, well evidently there's more to them than meets the eye. It's the green that counts."

I can see her smile. It's all over the room, written in the darkness.

She says: "Here take this home. You and your wife can have it for supper. Tell her I'd love to meet her. I think she must be a really nice lady."

I say: "You and Dennis, maybe you should get together." Then I think: Yes, maybe that's the answer. Bags in common.

She hands me two things – a piece of liver in a plastic bag, and in another tiny plastic bag a small brownish bit of stuff.

She says: "Why, who's Dennis?"

"Nobody. I was just thinking. In fact he's no one at all." Which must constitute some form of important breakthrough. Then I say: "Well thank you. The little bag looks interesting, what's in that?"

"That's a present for you. It's like, it's some sort of herb. I'd have it before you go to bed. You'll enjoy it."

64

Thick dusk. I'm halfway up the track when I hear this soft-padded lope panting up behind. I think: Christ! and glance back. It is, it's the hell-hound. Probably thinks I'm making off with his dinner. He stops and looks me over and snuffles a baleful of thick dusk. And then starts back towards the cottage as if on reflection I'd hardly be worth the bother.

I'm thinking: Hang on, how did Corny get her number? The plot thickens. Especially since it's now virtually proved he's hand in glove with Caruso.

4
PUTREFACTIO

65

Dark when I get home. I'm so tired I can hardly haul myself up the steps. I'm thinking: Better not let them see how exhausted I am – they might get the wrong idea. I try to straighten my hair. But that makes me feel that I do feel guilty. I rough it up again.

There's a light in the kitchen. I think: Fiona, and it'll be warm. I don't feel tired any more. Then I'm thinking excitedly: Time I came clean about SM. And there's so much to tell, like for instance...

For some reason all I can remember at this moment is the green knickers. And that's something I'm not certain I'm ready to tell about yet. Even Fiona.

66

A note beside the electric kettle.

So where have you been this time? Anyway we've all been having a really great time. See you when we get in – A. PS. We need to talk.

All... What does she mean they've all been having such a great time? I know what 'all' means. All means Dennis.

Now I feel utterly spent. So much for all my progress. I'm back chewing my lower lip. I'm back to square one.

I'm putting the piece of liver on a plate in the fridge when I think: I need a drink, a strong one. Maybe this is the moment to take the stuff SM gave me.

When I've dropped it from its little bag into the palm of my hand I think: What do I do, infuse it? Smoke it? Swallow it whole? I swallow it whole.

Somehow I've made it up the stairs. Without taking my clothes off I lie on our bed. The smell of me's appalling, like a tanner's garbage bin. Not that I can do anything about it at the moment. The dark is behaving in an odd way. It's going around, punctuated by light. The feeling I get is that I'm in a hammock, swinging, suspended inside something like a tumble-drier.

67

But it's blanket dark in the... in the tiny bedroom no bigger than a cupboard. I'm on my feet in the thick darkness. I can hear the blue-black fellow grinding his teeth, but am not certain his mind's on the job, sounds distracted as if maybe he's found something choice to gnaw.

It's cupboard dark. I wish he'd concentrate because I'm going to need him. This form of fear can undo you. Can find as many ways in as water.

I am, I'm steely, I'm looking around. I see the thing or rather because it's so dark I detect it – a cringing underdeveloped idiot sort of thing, a sort of abashed Dennis one could almost begin to pity. If it weren't for this scunner. One could almost forgive it if it weren't for the stinking fear. He conjures a fear that's not normal, it's elemental yellowy-brown with blinds beginning to flap and a faint cardamom smell. You breathe it and it breathes you. And you're blotted out completely.

I think: Enough's enough. I get up. I don't really know where the hell I am. I look round and see in the moonlight the damned pillow glow as if sick, and it is the fear. Horrible, shapeless, threatening.

A snarl, and together we've pounced.

In go the knees. My fingers and thumbs can explore each other through the pinched windpipe. I think: Okay enough's enough. But still, and still in this cupboard-sized room, fear stays alive. I try not to run out of the room. The fear follows me on tiptoe. And across the next room. And the next.

I don't know where I've gone. Or where the hell I am.

68

Another Bad Dream. I'm in the kitchen. Either I am having this dream or I really am back in the kitchen or I've always been in the kitchen but have been dreaming I was up in the bedroom or the cupboard or wherever the hell.

Anyway I'm in the kitchen. Thank God Fiona's with me. I'm in a stew because the glass of poison she put out is empty and I'm pretty certain it's me who's drunk it. I feel groggy and confused because after all we're not in the kitchen – we're in bed together.

As a matter of fact I'm deteriorating very fast. There are fizzing electric sensations running up and down my body and I can't turn them off.

I think: Monkeys – they're too quick for me and too strong.

I'm trying to get hold of Fiona when I think: Christ, intruders! Out on the terrace.

I'm rigid with fear. I hear one of them coming up the stairs, stop on the landing. Fiona and I tiptoe to the bedroom door. The dark is cupboard black. Fiona opens the door. The horror person is round the corner in the dark stairwell.

I think: Okay this is it. I growl, none too confidently, and then I'm out there facing him. Yes, there he is in... Oh, so now it's not the stairwell he's in, it's the cupboard.

Would you believe it – shacked-up in the cupboard, that same faceless horror. I leap right in on top of him – the scunner so strong in me I've gone berserk. He just yields like some chintzy sort of cushion. There's no smashing him. He is, he's indestructible.

69

Back in bed. Awake. Or perhaps not. This dark's unreal, a drape draped over the bed.

Fiona's there thank God or I'd be done for. From the inky water around the bed the monkey keeps reaching up and grabbing at bits of me with his fizzing electric fingers.

This doesn't feel like any sensible sort of dream.

70

SM says: "Try not shoving it away okay? Try, like, opening yourself to it."

I honestly don't know whether she said that or not. Or where I am or whether I'm dreaming or what the hell, but it seems a damn fool suggestion except that... except that everything has begun to change.

SM gives a slow contented sniff and then says dreamily as if she's far away and her mind's really on this cake she's baking: "See, easy! Now you see why you weren't getting anywhere fast. Like you were trying to lift yourself off the floor by pulling up your pants. Correction, I mean your knickers."

She chuckles sleepily. She's pleased with that. But I'm not really listening. I'm thinking: What on earth have they done to it? So I do, I give it a hug the poor squit of a little timid sort of Dennisy thing, undernourished, kept in a cupboard fiddling with himself. I pick it up. I hold the pillow in my arms and feel its relief like the first slap of clean air after the scarifying business of being born.

SM says: "Poo, it's rank in here. Maybe it's begun to happen – you've gone off. Maybe finally you're on the turn."

I look round. The blinds are flapping. I wait a moment before I feel sure. I'm sure.

I don't feel afraid.

71

Then something extraordinary. I'd not noticed the cold but it must be or we wouldn't have drawn the blue velvet curtain across the alcove in our bedroom. It's dark and there's a strenuous sort of activity going on behind the curtain.

I lie there in bed wondering whether I should cough, like we did at school when we'd catch the creak from Gibbon's cubicle and know there he was again surreptitiously tossing himself of.

Nothing surreptitious about this. I'm thinking: Surely not, surely she wouldn't... I mean, not here in my own bedroom, not when... when everything goes silent, apart from the rapidly abating storm of breathing.

Then comes the voice, sickeningly satisfied: "So what is conceived of our dark exalted and matching lust is the child cynocephalus..."

I'm thinking: Cornelius, he's got a damn nerve. Who asked him round? I'll soon shut him up. But I'm beginning to learn this Corny takes some stopping once he's bitted-up.

He goes aloofly on: "*Simia Dei*, the ape of God, whose anterior knowledge predates the flood, who can shin up the arbour philosophica and from the top branches can fix on the sun an eye open to every question. O, this is something not realized but its essence is of the transforming substance which is on the one hand extremely common even contemptible and on the other of great value, not to say divine. For this transformation may lead from the depths to the heights, and from the bestially archaic and infantile to the mystical *homo maximus*."

Well I've heard him out. Grrr, I'll give him homo maximus! I feel there are a couple of things Corny and I need to clarify. One being the nature of our relationship. Another: just what the hell he's up to. And that's without taking on board the Caruso dimension.

But not now because his voice has had a bad effect on me. I'm itching all over. At the same time I'm growling and snarling in a fairly unmotivated sort of fashion – as if passing the time of day.

I'm up off the bed. I'm thinking: I think I fancy a banana or something. I'm stalking-it lordly back and forth on the carpet on all fours, head high, picking up my forearms stylishly. I am, I'm a baboon. No question. From nose-tip to blazing bum that's what I am. Not a big deal. I feel pretty chipper about it. I'm altogether open to being a baboon. Up and down, up and down and then some grooming time and a bit of tick-hunting.

I scratch, snarl at the sun a bit, snarl a bit at the shadows, push out my chest and flick my tool which springs back at me with gratifying stalkiness. I'm feeling solid. Homo maximus be damned, this time evolution has really come up with the goods.

And I'm thinking about that feeling when I start wondering just what the hell it all adds up to and find I've relapsed into a deepening meditative peace.

72

Another Dream (possibly also bad). Fiona and I have been invited to a party. I go on ahead. There's a room beside the main room that I seem to be drawn into. Sitting over in the corner is – it is, it's going to be another bloody nightmare – Dennis.

I say: "How're things?" I'm feeling on top of the situation and quite well disposed towards him.

Dennis smiles. He says he's feeling temperamental.

I think: Temperamental, for griefsake! But at the same time I'm looking at him closely and trying to figure how I feel. Maybe he is improving, maybe he is getting to look a bit more like me. Anyway I feel almost unafraid of this thing of his with Fiona.

Then extraordinary: his girlfriend (yes, yet another girlfriend) comes in and settles herself comfortably in his lap, and at the same time I realize that Fiona has arrived and is standing behind me very close.

I ask Dennis this odd question: How is his garden coming on?

Dennis says he's been working in it and that I should see the size of his potatoes.

Potatoes? Potatoes! His girlfriend, whom I think of as Jennie even though she's much older than he is and dark-skinned and clearly something to do with Ayah, says: "And you should see how his physique is developing." At which Dennis is up and stripping off his shirt and displaying his torso. I think: He could be getting out of hand.

So I say: "If you were now to come off the beer you'd be quite a decent shape."

At which the formidable girlfriend rounds on me and says I'm insensitive to forget how in his childhood Dennis had this injury to overcome. She says: "On the contrary he's doing wonderfully well."

I think: Quite right, why ever would I want to put Dennis down? Which makes me think: Blimey, whatever's happened to you. Meaning me.

Fiona has gone to join the main party in the other room. I follow her and pass a sideboard loaded with eats. The centre of the spread is a cold, wonderfully garnished salmon-trout. I take a good look.

In quite a brilliant way from out of the mayonnaise he's eyeing me. He's raw and river-fresh. Know what, he's breathing. He's holding his mouth as if he's about to ogle a bubble but instead he seems to hiccup and out on the plate spills my wedding ring.

73

Going Into It. I'm lying in the dark, feeling really together and congratulating myself on what must have been an excellent dream – Dennis and the Fish.

Suddenly SM's back on the air.

I think: Wait a minute, it was probably her who was behind the curtain with Corny. Yes, that would explain a lot. Sex – that's usually what's at the back of it.

She says: "Go on then, go into that."

"Into what?"

"Whatever it is go into it."

This is a new twist.

"I don't know that I want to go into any damn thing ever again."

"Fine, so go into that, right?"

But I'm thinking: Maybe after all, there is something I'd quite like to go into. But I don't know what SM would think. She might wash her hands of the whole business. Then, very distant, very poor reception she says: "Something's turning you on, right? So go into that."

I say: "Fine for you but it's not that easy."

I lie there in the dark a minute. Undecided. At the same time I know I've already made up my mind. I get up off the mattress and feel my way in the dark. Ah, here we go.

What I go into is the cupboard.

I was right – it's not so easy. That's because the floor's ankle-deep in shoes, mostly high-heeled.

Fiona's cupboard.
Which is the cupboard I was keen to go into.

74

The Cupboard. What I keep saying is: "Mmmmm."

In here it's another sort of dark. Airless. One feels all gloved-up in it. Squatting here among the high heels I can tell I'm content. I've really arrived. This is very definitely where I'm at.

I nose about, burrow around with my head, encounter all sorts of cool softnesses, soft warmnesses and warm clingy things. I take my time, which isn't surprising since when one's arrived where one's really at one, one's into forever.

Dreamily I move from cràpe de chine to mousseline encountering every sort of privacy and vague scent that make the airless dark full of colour, twilight colours, earth-after-the-rain scents, the sort of scents you get from huge fleshy white flowers with sticky pistols. *Lillium candidum*. Here in the dark I have the feeling I'm competing with hundreds of switched-on moths. I can feel the brush of moth wings on my cheeks, a dusting of eyelids, the touch of...

75

Sporting Event. I'm next in the ring. Actually I've already fought a couple of rounds against a diminutive opponent with a look of... Bernard Levin – who's flagrantly bending the rules by fighting in his spectacles.

At present I'm waiting to get back in the ring and finish the contest. Longing for it. Feeling really confident, really on song.

But first I must get changed.

Immediately I'm tense. I've had trouble with this 'changing' bit before. Like the time I was asked to turn out for The Rotarians, and the night before dreamed I was getting padded-up against the Australians only to find my bag was full of primary school pads – all of them left-leg. Mike Brearly, bearded and glaring like William Blake's God the Father in furious aspect, promoted someone in the order to take my place. Whom did I watch stride purposefully out of the Long Room into the sunlight, the deafening applause and Wisden's? Brian Telfont.

And now here we go again. I'm back in the changing-room looking for one of my trainers. No good, I reckon someone's nicked it. At which moment as if bang on cue Brian Telfont breezes in flush from the ring and wearing something like a cross between the Lonsdale Belt and an outsize ornate leather and brass protector.

Hullo, my sister's here too.

I think: I don't think I've ever met my sister before. Actually I didn't know I had a sister. Surely though, she'd know better than ever to be a girlfriend of Telfont. But she's furious with me, which seems to figure.

She says: "When are you going to acknowledge my presence?" And storms out leaving me wondering what she was doing making her presence felt in the men's changing room in the first place.

I'm still searching for my trainer. I think: Right pad, right trainer, always it's the right one that's missing. I'm becoming desperate, so frustrated my eyes are pricking frustration tears like glass splinters.

I'm thinking: I have, I've missed my chance in the ring – when suddenly over in the corner I see her sock. I think: That's going to have to do. But as I go to put it on it somehow changes, becomes sheer, becomes I don't know, something really feminine like sheer tights, and putting my foot in it and then getting it up over my shin I think: Crumbs, and hey just a minute, hang on. HANG ON!

Before I'm able to get a grip on things, there, it's happened: I've been and gone and... I'm sodden.

I think: That's not only absolutely disgusting it's the last thing one wants to happen before a big fight. I won't have any... any spunk left for the ring.

Anyway for better or worse I'm now kitted-out. Very much aware of these sticky tights I set out for the stadium. It seems it's speechday or something, hell of a big deal.

I find one of the masters at the back of the hall. I say: "Look I've still got to finish my fight."

Know who this master is? It's Field Marshall Montgomery. He looks me over disapprovingly – could be my tights though I am doing my best, holding my knees together and that.

Monty says that I'm too late, I've missed it. I think: Oh no, some things you don't get out of that easily.

I say: "Look, I've simply got to get this fight finished, tell me how can it be arranged?"

Monty says: "You're going to have to discuss this with the authorities when you get back to England."

I say: "England! – so where am I for Christsake?"

Monty looks at me quizzically and then as if this is going to come as a shock to me he says: "Canada."

It does – comes as a hell of a shock.

76

I'm awake am I? Takes a moment to identify this particular dark. Ah yes, the cupboard. The word Canada is on my tongue.

I attend to this. A fragment or two, and then in an avalanche the entire dream and more and more of it comes sliding back.

I think: Acutely disturbing, but at the same time you can see I'm making real progress – I'm beginning to sense: which are the really knotty questions. For instance this one: What the devil's Canada got to do with it? I know about Penang but... Only one person can answer this. Corny.

Uncanny, no sooner the thought than the whole cupboard goes down with the smell of belched onion.

Corny says: "Pretty obvious. Canada's the place on the other side of the Atlantic."

"You mean, Oh I see, the Atlantic."

"Yes, ever heard of it? The Big Deep? No? Then I don't suppose you ever heard of The New World."

I'm beginning to dislike Corny.

He says: "So your problem's this side of the ocean. Back here in England, in the old world, with the authorities. The old world authorities. Get it?"

"No."

For a minute I keep a sulky silence. I'm determined to have no further truck with Corny. But then I hear someone, in fact I suspect it's me, say: "Okay Paracelsus, now tell me why it's always my right pad that's missing?"

"Same thing." He breaks into a jingle: "Problem's back in England. No you don't get it do you? Listen. Your left pad's a bit of a tight fit, right? Now find your right pad and you'll also have consciousness sorted out. Consciousness sorted out equals conscious protection. For conscious and unconscious protection you need something reliable in the middle. In other words, don't go out to bat against the quick boys without wearing a box. He, he, he."

"Why's that funny?"

"Your protector. You don't get it, do you?"

I'm having an idea. I don't know whether to mention it.

I say carelessly: "Probably a bit far-fetched to see too much connection between my lost wedding ring and this boxing-ring. I mean the boxing-ring's square."

I've scored. Corny gives a whistle. Astonishment? Approval? I don't know but the whistle draws itself out, begins to crack and then to crackle – and then it's atmospherics in the background of Corny's latest proclamation: "The circle is called mediator, making peace between enemies or opponents or opposites or the four elements. Nay, rather he alone effects the squaring of the circle. Opposites meet as bride and groom together in one circle, you could no longer recognize what was outside or inside, or lower and upper, but all would be one thing in one circle or vessel. For this vessel is the true philosophical pelican, and there is no other to be sought for in all the world."

I say: "Christus!"

"Amen to that," says Corny.

"I mean," I say, "we're back to the pelican. The heron!"

"Who's a bright boy?"

Sometimes I don't know how I put up with Corny.

"But that was when I lost my ring. So is there any indication here of where I might find it?"

He's begun to laugh.

"Didn't you mention the providence of the Resurrective Fish, the great King Salmon?" He can hardly get it out he's laughing so much. "But first you've still got one whole round to complete. In the ring. In the square ring. Quite a joke, isn't it?"

There's a click – over and out. I'm left in the cupboard – in the dark.

77

I'm starting to laugh. A bit tentative at first. A bit as if it might be on top of the whinges. But then it's getting the hang of itself, is coming up through itself like a turbulence of clear water coming up from the bottom of a murky pond. Coming in waves. Wave on wave.

There in the cupboard as I rock backwards and forwards, and hug myself against the agony of the laughter, the silky things, all the cool satins, they rain down on me off their hangers. I laugh hopelessly and helplessly.

I laugh till I think: If I don't stop laughing I'll do myself a permanent mischief.

78

Ssh! I might have known it – dad!

I can hear him on his way up the stairs. If he catches me in the cupboard again there's bound to be a show-down. In fact a court marshal with full military honours.

No chance of him seeing the joke – especially if I've wet myself. But nothing, not even the thought of dad can stop me laughing.

The pain's killing me. I think I've ruptured my appendix. I can feel the tears pouring down my face. Each time I think maybe I'm getting a grip on myself I remember the joke – and I'm off again.

I suppose it was bound to happen, that I'd remember the joke just as the door of the cupboard was flung open.

79

Fiona says: "What are you doing? What on earth's up?"

I try to explain but the laughter has me jack-knifed and all I achieve is rolling out of the cupboard onto the carpet.

Fiona says: "Oh my God."

I wish she wouldn't say things like that. Anything that makes me laugh on top of what I'm already laughing at will be the end of me.

Fiona shrieks: "Oh no. I don't believe it. It's not true."

That's done it. Now I'll need intensive care. To make things worse she does something totally irresponsible. Her eyes which were on the cusp of grey go soft and blue and she begins to laugh.

Annabel's running up the stairs. She knocks on the door.

"What are you two up to, not that I want to know?"

"You'd better not come in," Fiona squawks as if she's being strangled. And then to reassure everyone that the situation isn't yet as critical as it conceivably might be she really begins to laugh. Cackles like a scurrilous old parrot.

Annabel shouts: "Come off it you two, what's going on?"

I manage to wail: "You don't understand because you're not in on the joke."

That's when Annabel comes in.

"OH MY GOD!" she says. One look at her and her gaping wide eyes points me to what I should have been looking at.

I say:"Oh my God."

I see what they mean. I hadn't realized it was for real. Where on earth did I find them anyway. I mean I didn't know Fiona had any green knickers.

80

For a moment I almost stop laughing. Then I see Fiona doubled-up, staggering around in little circles. I'm thinking: It's no good, this time I'm going to wet myself. And then I'm going to die.

Annabel says: "You ought to be ashamed of yourself. You could end up a dirty old man."

"Mumma!" I say.

"End up!" Fiona shrieks. She collapses on the bed and begins thrashing about.

Suddenly she sits up and starts tearing off her jumper.

"For God's sake mother, what do you think you're now doing?"

"I don't think, I know."

"You're just encouraging him."

"I'm not, I'm having a hot flush."

"Right, I'll leave the pair of you to it. You're as bad as each other. Worse actually."

I manage enough breath to squeak: "No, no you don't understand, you've not heard the joke."

Annabel stops in the doorway.

"It better be good."

I bite my lip. Finally I'm sufficiently in control. Syllable by syllable I lay it on the line.

"I couldn't find my right pad – and so missed my chance of a maiden ton against the Aussies."

"Very funny," says Annabel. She has this way of raising one eyebrow.

"You don't get it?" Maybe things are more serious than I'd thought. "See, it's all connected to the knickers. All I ever had to do was take them off. That's all. Just take them off."

"Not while I'm in the room you don't. Anyway you smell horrible – all meaty."

"That's right. I've been doing some butchery. Didn't you see the plate of liver in the fridge?"

Now she's raised the other eyebrow. Both eyebrows raised.

"You need a bath."

She goes out and emphatically shuts the door. She calls back. "Father, I need to have a word with you, but this isn't the moment."

I turn to Fiona who's sitting on the bed wiping her eyes. She's torn off practically everything.

I say: "You got it, didn't you?"

"I wasn't really listening. I was too hot."

I look at her, all hot-flushed and mopping up. Suddenly I'm thinking: She is, she's beautiful.

I don't say anything for a bit and then I say: "It sounds silly but I think I'm coming out the far end of something."

She gives a shriek and rolls back on the bed with her hands over her eyes.

I say: "I don't mean that, I mean coming out of the far end of this experience."

"So it's true. What's she like?"

"I thought you thought that. Absolutely not, what I've been doing is working on myself."

"I see," she says vacantly. "Actually I never really thought you had. Phew, it's hot."

I say: "I feel everything's beginning to fall into place."

She looks at me. I think: Oh no, she's going to start laughing again. But she doesn't.

I say: "Fiona, you know I really do love you. I've always known it, but now I know I know it."

"I love you," she says.

But then she looks me up and down. She begins to smile, and then she says: "Oh my God."

That's done it. That's set the pair of us laughing again.

5
THE BATH

81

Definite Progress. A cold breath on my forehead. I open my eyes. Fiona's already up, the curtains already drawn, the sky so steely blue it's almost colourless. The light is icicle brilliant.

I've made it, clear as a bell. I could almost weep – the sheer pain-joy of being in touch with this first-thing-in-the-morning happiness I used always to feel. Head to toe, no one's messing me about.

I submit to the Caruso test. There you go – still perfectly composed. Amazing.

82

I'm remembering a dream: Know whose place this is? Dennis's. I've called on him in his scruffy little terrace house. He isn't in. Thank God for that. In fact it's my impression he's moved out. I decide I'll do the decent thing and have a bath.

No sooner into it than in comes Dennis. He looks me out some soap and then he starts washing me. For some reason I feel really moved. I thank him.

He says: "You smell a bit meaty."

Which is what woke me. He's right, I do. I need a bath.

83

Bath. A good scrub. Then I lie back for a soak. Ours is a big bath. Take a deep breath and you can float.

I'm having this calm thought: Water doesn't hang about. Water is so much into everything, it's like it's the one feeling everywhere. Not like light because light casts shadows, has this other side to it. Water is complete, like perfect dark.

I'm not used to thinking like this – it feels like quite an event.

Then I'm thinking – at least I think I'm thinking, though by now I might just be dreaming. Anyway I'm thinking: Yes, but water stops at the skin – it's a surface experience... and then I realize I'm wrong. I can feel the water begin to fill me from my toes. Into my ankles, shins, through into my thighs. And from there... I can't describe the feeling. Whatever bit the water reaches just gasps and gives up. Just opens and becomes the feeling of the water. I wouldn't want to describe the feeling.

It's like becoming liquid, it's like giving up being fixed and becoming the feeling. When the water reaches my heart the opening comes as a sigh. When it reaches my throat, I hear, as if in the distance, a little cry. When it's up to my eyes I lose touch. Now I'm definitely dreaming.

I'm driving a blue dormobile which has a double bed in the back. Beside me is a little dark girl. She is wearing a green sari embroidered with violet eyes like the eyes on a peacock's tail. Between her eyebrows is painted a glowing crimson disc. In the past (that means the past I'm aware of in the dream) she would never speak to me, in fact never even look at me. Today it's quite different. Today she's not only smiling – she's holding my hand. I feel my heart go all warm and liquid. This is the sort of happiness they've been keeping from me.

I'm driving her to a Tudor manor house, heavily haunted, in the woods somewhere near where I was born. In the drive we meet the owner's tweedy, sensible wife. I'm surprised to find even she looks friendly. And then I recognise her – she's the sensible woman I've known all my life. I stop the dormobile and call to her: "I'm coming to show you my new girlfriend."

"That's nice," the woman says.

"And did you know that her name is Ayah?"

As I wake up I think: Well, if that isn't a turn-up for the books!

As I towel myself I catch sight of me in the mirror. It's a shock. Only one way to describe what I look like – I look rather... well, on song. Certainly nothing effeminate, but open and, in a manly sort of way, soft.

Don't some people say everyone, even presumably someone you'd think a dead loss from this point of view, someone like say Brian Telfont, has this other side?

Still it is a shock.

84

On my way back to the bedroom I run into Annabel. She stops and looks at me. It's her smile that comes as the next shock. She doesn't look as if she's smiling, but it's definitely around somewhere. The feeling's like that feeling an unsuccessful granny gets in a game of Grandmother's Footsteps. You look round and everyone's stone still and looking innocent enough, but writ large over the entire garden is a damn great smile. Everyone's in on some plot. In fact everyone's closing in.

I say: "Oh, hullo."

"You alright? You're looking really odd, kind of... beautiful.'

I think: What the hell's that supposed to mean. Does she think... Yes I know what she's thinking. Knickers.

"Can't stop. It'll have to wait till this evening." She shouts this from the stairs.

"What will?"

"I want a word with you, remember?" And the front door slams. It opens again. "Did mum tell you about the police?"

And slams again.

I think: Did she say police? Caruso!

85

I walk into the kitchen feeling vaguely prominent – this sense of being so to speak on song takes some getting used to.

Fiona's cooking porridge. She looks up.

I think: Wonderful, what a warm beautiful look. You'd certainly not guess on this showing she felt she was wasting her life.

In spite of my worry about the police, I'm aware I'm tremendously in love with her – which is more proof I really have come through. I'm looking at her and am, I'm pretty certain, managing to convey my come-throughness when suddenly she does something very annoying. She smiles. Not her good smile – it's *the* smile. All around her, like Annabel's.

I think: They're in this together. It was definitely a mistake letting them in – I mean on the knickers.

I say chillily: "Will you kindly tell me what's going on?"

"Is something going on?"

I think: That's crafty.

Fiona shrugs her shoulders and looks down at the porridge. The smile however continues to stare me in the face. And there's something else staring me in the face.

I say: "I suppose Dennis went with you last night?"

Fiona says: "Oh for goodness sake, I thought you thought you'd come through all that."

"Well I didn't know what you were smiling at."

"Nor did I. Or perhaps I did. You see you've got this new way of looking rather beautiful. Yes, as a matter of fact he did."

"What do you mean, he did?"

"Come with us last night. Dennis. It was a very happy evening."

And here was me thinking we'd got all that business finally sorted out. I say: "Good. Excellent. I'm glad you enjoyed yourself."

Fiona ignores this. She says: "He was with his new girlfriend."

I think: Another new girlfriend. He's like an epidemic. A Spanish Fly virus that's getting out of hand. Just when I think I've got the stopper on him he breaks out again somewhere else.

I say: "Who's it this time?"

She's looking in the saucepan and smiling as if she and the porridge are a secret society.

"They tell me it's all your doing."

"I beg your pardon?"

"The way you set them up. They think you're wonderful. The two of them make a lovely couple."

I'm hit by a feeling of appalling crisis. Annabel. She's had a change of heart. Surely she wouldn't do this to me?

I say: "Is that why she wants to speak to me?"

"Who?"

"Annabel."

"Not Annabel. Jennie."

"Jennie wants to speak to me! What about for Christsake?"

"I don't know. I didn't know Jennie wanted to speak to you."

I look at Fiona for a moment. Then I say: "You don't mean it, not Jennie!"

"Hullo, yes it's me," says Jennie, pushing in through the swing-doors. Trailing that same damned smile. I should have known she'd be in on it too.

I say: "You're fired."

Fiona says: "He's only joking."

I think: She's right. I'd better be joking. I've only to put a foot wrong and Dennis will be in possession of the green knickers. He'll be crowing all over the parish. And then it will be back to the Rotary.

Still I've succeeded in wiping the grin off her face. And off Fiona's. She glares at me and goes and starts mopping Jennie up.

I say: "Come on, only joking."

Fiona says: "Sometimes you go too far. If you would only pull yourself together we'd all be perfectly happy."

Me! So now it's me who's going too far. Not Dennis. Dennis is perfectly happy. Dennis can hump every female in the county. That wouldn't be going too far.

Jennie's looking up through her tears adoringly at Fiona.

She sniffs and says: "Would it be alright if Dennis brings his sandwiches round at lunchtime?"

Fiona says: "Yes love, of course it would."

That does it. I say: "The curate too. He's bringing his sandwiches. Ham."

They're both looking at me. I've gone too far. I say: "Come on, ha, ha, ha. Only joking. I'm not going to be here anyway."

"Where are you going?" That's Fiona. I find this sudden shrill of suspicion intensely gratifying. "You're always popping out."

Jennie says: "Yes, always popping out."

Vicious little bitch.

I look at Fiona and say airily: "Me? I'm just off to pull myself together. I think I've still a bit more work to do. I've not come through quite as far as I thought."

Fiona waits till I reach the door and then says: "You mean, back in the cupboard."

In front of Jennie... how could she? That's a terrible betrayal. I turn. We glare at each other for a minute, and then something extraordinary happens. She's begun to smile. The smile hits me like a summer morning.

She says: "Phew, it's getting hot!" Hot flush. She starts undoing her blouse.

I think: Dear God we're so lucky knowing we do trust each other. Implicitly.

As I push out through the swing doors I hear me say: "I don't know, I'm really nuts about you."

"Nuts is the word," Fiona says. A bit muffled, but that's because she's got her blouse stuck over her head.

Jennie is looking doe-eyed and beginning to cry again. I hear her sob ecstatically: "Oh when he looks like that he looks just like my Dennis."

Fiona shouts: "Did Annabel tell you about the police?"

86

I'm driving along the main road, thinking: Probably I should have contacted the police, but on top of everything else...

I take a look at myself in the driving mirror. No significant change, that same buffed-up open look. Well, it's good to be open, isn't it? Receptive.

I'm overtaken by a white plumber's van, going like the clappers. I catch a glimpse of the driver.

"Hey!" I think. Wasn't that Caruso? He's doing a runner."

A quick check in the mirror. Open? I look tight as a clam. A clamped clam, a pale one. As I approach the lay-by before the turn-off to SM's something at the side of the road flaps in the breeze as if trying to attract my attention.

It does attract my attention.

I think: Outrageous! You never know who might be out for a stroll. Children, old ladies, or people who shouldn't have to be exposed to this sort of thing. Like nuns.

I stop in the lay-by, walk back and pick the thing up.

Just as I suspected. One of *those* magazines. So fresh it could have been jettisoned by Caruso to speed his get away. What I'll do is put it in the litter bin in the lay-by. Which I'm about to do when I think: Maybe I should take a quick look in case it could be evidence for the prosecution. Or... or the defence. And besides it's important I know once and for all what they get up to in this sort of magazine.

Good Lord!

It is, it's disgraceful.

I'm checking through the pages to see just how disgraceful things can get when another car pulls up in the lay-by. Hey, suppose it's one of my clients! Suppose it's a member of the Rotary. I don't look round. I stuff the thing in the litter bin and walk fairly nonchalantly back to my car whistling.

I'm whistling 'Kiss Me In The Rain.' But I don't suppose that has any particular significance.

Then I look round. It's a police car.

88

The cottage door's shut. I've knocked. Maybe she's not in. But that would surprise me. There's an odd secretive air over the place, as if it's holding it's breath hoping I'll go away. I look around. For some reason I begin to think again about the magazine. I still feel incensed. I mean what some girls are prepared to get up to. Let alone be photographed doing. There should certainly be a law.

Phew. Actually I feel quite disturbed about it.

I take a step back. Behind the upstairs windows the curtains are half-drawn. I think: That's odd.

And then I think: It's this place that's disturbing me – there's something odd about it. Then I hear someone coming. The door's being unlocked. That's odder than odd, the fact she's chosen to lock it. The door opens a few inches.

SM says: "Oh it's only you. I thought you might be the police. What do you want?"

I say: "Police! Me? No, I was on the verge of an important breakthrough. Actually this will interest you, I was in the bath..."

"You mean you took that stuff I gave you?"

"Yes, delicious. What was it?"

"You put the police onto us, didn't you?"

"Us? No I didn't. Actually they're onto me too. They could be following me."

I don't know why I say that. And anyway what does she mean *us*? Hang about – does she mean...?

"Hey! Caruso wasn't up there just now, was he?"

"Who?" she says, a bit airily, I think. "No, that was the plumber."

"A plumber! You mean a leak!"

She looks at me suspiciously. Then closes the door.

I think: What the hell's going on? The fact is she looks different – she's got black liner around her eyes. Maybe she's doing an incognito. Maybe she's on the run. And the way she held the door. Virtually shut. Maybe... maybe she didn't have any clothes on. Then I'm thinking: You know what it is, it's drugs. The Caruso connection. Fiona was right.

Then the door opens again.

89

SM says: "Come on in then quick, what you waiting for?"

I'm not waiting. What I'm doing is thinking: Now wait a minute!

"Buck up, it's cold!"

Well it would be if you're wearing just (I could be wrong about the 'just' but for some reason I don't think so) a crocheted dressing-gown. Flame red. She's closed the door and is sitting one cheek on the table like someone who is busy and doesn't want to be all day. She has her arms folded which keeps her dressing-gown from coming open. She's crossed her legs. Now here's something I'd not have believed, and which proves I was wrong about the 'just.' She's wearing stockings or tights or something. Black. She gives her hair a shake, that way women do who are used to being looked at. And then she looks at me.

I don't feel at ease and that's the truth. I'm looking around and I feel I could at any moment regress and start to chew my bottom lip. What's she done to the place? It's all tidied up and bare. Where's she put the green lentils, the black-eyed beans? The only thing on the dresser's a pile of old telephone books. And a glass of disgusting-looking sort of bloody custard.

She says: "Strong stuff. You should have a glass. Do you good."

I say: "Yes, well what is it?"

"Beestings. It's the first milk, got blood in it. It makes your hair stand on end. And, though it might not interest you, that's just for starters."

I look back at her. I'm pretty sure I see her adjust her expression. She'd been watching me with a shared-secret smile. I've had enough of these smiles for one day – I'm never the one whose sharing the secret. Now she's looking hard and disinterested.

She says: "Okay, so fetch the mattress. Get a move on, I'm expecting another client."

That's when I hear a movement upstairs. I'd say it was definitely a bedspring. Followed by the silence of someone who's got his head stuffed in a pillow so as not to laugh out loud. I've glanced at the ceiling. Then quickly back to SM – hard as nails. But it could be it's her way of managing not to laugh.

I have this sudden certainty she's got someone tucked away up there.

She says: "Well do you want the mattress or don't you?"

90

I'm lying with my knees up letting the breathing do the... well, actually it seems to be holding its breath. That's the moment the bedsprings sigh again.

I think: This is outrageous. Thoroughly unprofessional. I mean, in the middle of the day! Still that proves it. Women! Know what I'd like to do to women? I'd like to grrr...

This time I'll take care of them all. The whole package, including the bits they keep shut away in the bathroom cupboard, and in their handbags, and those things in their drawers. Yuk!

91

SM's (would you believe it?) lit a cigarette. She's still sat at the table, her arms folded keeping her dressing-gown more or less, not altogether, together. She's looking at me curiously. The joke's still twitching around her mouth so I guess she's still on the hotline to... this is unbelievably humiliating.

SM says: "What was that you were doing?"

"Who me?"

She uncrosses her legs and crosses them the other way.

"What were you doing?"

As a matter of fact I've now finished what I was doing and am wiping my hands on my... on my brown dungarees.

Dungarees?

SM snaps: "Your last chance – What were you doing?"

I feel the red run scalding into my cheeks, and prick the back of my neck. Then I hear myself say: "I've stuffed it all in the bin."

That does it. There's a sound from upstairs as if someone's fallen out of bed. I glance up, then back to SM. She's pretending the smoke's got in her eyes. But I know better, I know the two of them have this joke going. She's trying not to laugh. Finally she says unsteadily: "Fine, well you'd better go into that hadn't you?"

I say: "How, I mean how does one go into...?"

"Just, you know, go into it."

"You mean, do you, into the litter bin?"

Upstairs whoever it is has fallen out of bed again and is heaving around. Suddenly SM gets vicious: "I'll say you fucking go into it. If that's where you thought you could dispose of her, that's where you fucking well better be prepared to go. How else you going to get her back? Or do you really think you can get on without her? Shit, some men... it makes you sick!"

I think: I've had this up to here. Maybe I'll just walk out.

Then I think: Nope, I'm in such a mess and any minute the police are going to show up – I'd better give it a go. So I lie back. But it seems the breathing doesn't want to do the breathing.

What it seems it does want to do is a bit of... deep breathing.

92

A wind's picking up again. Storm-force. I'm thinking of the monsoon, of the fizzing monkeys on the roof.

I'm in a room, the storm's outside and there's a big threat from 'things' (I can't put it clearer than that) – they want to come in.

I'm into a period of horrible electrical heeby-jeebs – sweeping right through my body. Almost certainly to do with the monkeys.

I'm making these odd weird cries – little fearful hopeful whoops and howls.

I'm wondering: I wonder if there's something in me that's calling to those monkeys. I'm not, am I, about to invite them in?

93

Then the big storm moves inside. I'm the one who's being swept away. I'm being stretched as if something, perhaps the torrent, is hauling at my feet.

I'm reaching out, I think for somebody's hand. It's then I see the pair of them up on the bank, sleek, she in a scarlet satin evening dress, he in an over-egged, be-medalled red mess kit, menacingly red, chatting away.

My voice doesn't carry to them out of the torrent, or else they ignore it. Now they've turned their backs and are walking away into the trees.

"Who?"

My mum and someone pretending to be my dad!

Anyway they're gone, the pair of them. Clear out of the picture.

The white-crusted water topples me out of sight. I'm sunk, swallowed up by the yellow flood-watery half-light. The race is not only cutting me adrift and to bits, it's tearing me wide open. The water smells and tastes like liquid earth.

No option but to open up and breathe the stuff.

94

The Lion and the Unicorn. I've dreamed, let me see, it's about Fiona taking me into this grotty Italian hotel. I'm excited, it's a nice place to spend the night. It may have a faded front but I know it's exclusive. As if to prove it the door's opened by an Italian girl who could be Claudia Cardinale. She seems to know Fiona, leads us through the foyer, through a dingy firedoor and there it is, the smart country club, crowds of people, clearly a big do.

We have tea with Fiona's aristocratic female relations. We all stand up, we're on the move. I stand back thinking I'll nick one last chocolate biscuit. When I look round Fiona's gone.

Trying to find her I go down some wide stone stairs that lead underground. I'm in a vast hushed park, golden, late-summer and everywhere there are crowds drifting as if part of some gigantic fete.

I think: This is like the Elysian fields. There's a stir in the crowd. They cheer in a hushed down-in-the-wind sort of way, and there along the chestnut avenue comes the cavalcade. Bands, horseguards – and finally, what's this? A towering carnival float peopled with gaudy animals. But these aren't effigies. Look at the glinting brown animal eyes, these are for real.

This is the triumph of the Lion and the Unicorn. I can catch their zooey smell. They glance here and there, alert for any movement in the crowd. I wouldn't trust them an inch. I wander on through the underworld of stalls and salons, sleepy violin music, picnics on the grass.

I'm looking for Fiona. I'm depressed that I can't find her.

95

I open my eyes. Hullo, SM's moved. In fact I think she's gone. I'm pretty sure she's gone, but I'm too sleepy to be bothered to sit up and check for sure. She's probably upstairs. The pair of them's probably... probably done a runner.

The phone's ringing. By the sound of it, a very urgent call.

I jump up and run to the shelf by the door. There's a problem – I can see that, even if I am just out from a deep sleep. The problem is someone's removed the phone. Forcibly. The cord's still there, with its ends naked.

The ringing continues with increasing urgency.

I look around. Could she, I wonder, have had the phone moved upstairs? The bell sounds closer than that – so close it might be inside one's own head.

Ah, someone's answered it. Wait a minute... it's for me. Or at any rate I can hear his voice as if I had my ear on the receiver. A disembodied séance-creepy voice. Corny's.

I think: This is a trick. He sounds somewhere close by, behind a screen or in a bottle or... No, surely not. That couldn't be Corny she's got, or had tucked away in the upstairs room? That plus the Caruso connection – it would be tantamount to a can of worms.

I'd prefer not to hear what Corny has to say. I find the situation distasteful. I go back and lie down, put my hands over my ears. But when he's in this mood there's no stopping him. I hear every word.

"...Now he makes haste to bind and betroth himself to the virgin bride," he sounds breathless and disgustingly full of ardour, "and to get her with child in the bath over a moderate fire. But the virgin will not become pregnant at once unless she is kissed in repeated embraces."

I don't believe it – now there's the sound of bed springs. After a bit he continues: "Then she conceives in her body, and thus is begotten the child of good omen, in accordance with the order of nature. Then will appear in the bottom of the vessel the mighty Ethiopian, burned, discoloured, altogether dead and lifeless. He asks to be buried, to be sprinkled with his own moisture and slowly calcined till he shall arise in glowing form from the fierce fire. Because of the bath of renewal he takes a new name..."

After a moment there's a click. And then the dialling tone.

96

My Girlfriend. I'd say I'm about ten. I can feel the between-times peace of it, the summery lying-back on my back on my bed and my body stretching himself, alive (especially in the midriff and in the smokey lightning flavour of the breathing) to these assured new flutterings, tremblings and dense shadowy green sensations...

In SM's kitchen the winter light is warm and high summer. My eyes are open. I know exactly where I am. But what I breathe is this... this other independent ten year old's summery light.

The door has opened. She's come in. Ten-ish, meaning about my age. Blond, the hair with a freckle-red summer sandiness, free and chunky on her shoulders.

One part of me scrutinizes her, trying to figure out where the look of Fiona is set. The light is licking around the room, that's the light that's in my breath. It's in her also so that there's a gleam to her.

I think: that's the gleam of things that are certain.

She catches sight of me, and stops. She smiles and puts her hand on her chest as if to say I startled her. Still smiling she wrinkles her nose in some sort of puzzlement. Her smile is asking: "What's up this time?"

I look away and the wimp in me chokes: "Just the thought that in a minute you might choose to walk out on me or something."

She scratches and shakes her head at the same time, and laughs and says: "Oaf. That's French for a rotten egg. That's what you are. Can't you see we're friends. What they call inseparable. Can't you feel it?"

Her green eyes look me a strange look, in one way still and penetrating, in another dancing and mischievous and I feel everything inside me begin to scramble. Her eyes don't let me go – and yet I see all of her. See her move. Yellow dungarees, white shirt, white knickers, deftly she's out of them. She runs over and kneels on the mattress.

She says: "Now can you see?"

She's, well, she's perfect. Perfectly together. I know only that one day the happiness I feel won't any longer feel like a pain – I'll be able to breathe freely, like breathing light. I mean this light that's within the light. Like the green light in her eyes.

97

Maybe we're a little older. There are reasons for supposing this. We've been talking – and whatever we talk about it feels we're talking about everything – when all of a sudden I realize she's said it, she's said she's going to be with me, always has been and always will be, but that I'm going to have to understand that she has her own life to lead. That's something I'm going to have to live with. In other words, be alive to. If you're not alive to something then you're dead to it. She says that in a whisper, as if it's our secret.

I'm looking at her and thinking: No sweat, just now I feel alive to everything.

98

The cottage daren't believe what's happening. It's holding its breath. I'm not.

I'm aware that the loudest sound hereabouts is my slow, contented breathing.

I'm thinking: Yes, alive to everything – she's like my experience of the thing I discovered in Fiona.

Then I think: Fiona's my love, right? That means she's the embodiment of what I'm alive to. But if I'm no longer alive to anything, I mean if I've got to feeling it's all humdrum and deadly and heading for the grave, then she's landed with being the embodiment of what I'm dead to. It's up to me.

I feel I can't wait. I must get home and share with Fiona this pearl I've come up with. I suddenly think: I love her so much I'd like to leap and flick out my hind legs like a mad hare.

Quiet as I can I put the mattress and cushions back in their cupboard. Then I look around. The cottage feels somehow deserted. In fact I wouldn't swear to it they'd not, the two of them, gone. Nevertheless I tiptoe out, and using both hands I close the front door without a sound.

That's been good work. I bet SM would think so too. I'm probably through now. I probably won't be back. Shame I wasn't able to say goodbye.

99

I'm turning into the main road thinking I should perhaps drive out to Besseldon Manor and check the completed conservatory, and then thinking maybe it would be sensible first to call by at the Police Station and give myself up – when someone snatches the wheel. It's as if a highjacker had slipped violet shades over my eyes, before he grabs hold of my wrists.

Maybe the truth is that I'm party to what's happening, but I still reckon it would take someone of the calibre of Ignatius Loyola to judge which one of us is in control.

I'm slowing down, crossing the road and there, I've fetched up in the lay-by. Whatever this is I'm alive to, it's got me trembling and has clearly made up my mind.

Out of the car, padding across the tarmac to the litter bin.

I think: Ah, I see now, of course I just needed to check up precisely what it was I chucked away in the litter bin. Yuk, smells like the municipal tip in a heatwave. But I see what I'm after. Or so I think.

What I actually reach down for and come up with turns out to be a sheet of the local paper. I'm about to chuck it away when my eye's collared. It's the inside page.

Know what it is?

It's the list of deaths, marriages and births.

I hesitate. I don't know what the hell to think.

It's at this point I look round. The police car, another police car is parked there at the back of the lay-by. In the driving seat there's one hell of a policeman with a ginger moustache who's watching me while he talks into what looks like somebody's headphone.

I think: I'd better get the hell out of here. And as if getting shot of the swag, I stuff the Deaths, Marriages and Births page back in the litter bin.

100

As I drive on home I'm thinking: I feel shook up. I was fine, completely together, but now I feel I've been thrashed by demons.

Late afternoon, dull, the day's already knocked off.

Soon as I'm out of the car I feel a stillness or silence or something loitering in the garden like a gang of train-robbers.

Inside the front door I shout. Seems no one's at home.

I think: Just as well. That's because I'm already on my way up the stairs. I'm not sure where I'm going but I could make an informed guess.

101

Here in the cupboard, just to recap. Not of course a compulsive re-run, but the approach from the opposite direction, which is what SM said is essential.

Ah, here we go. There's this cosy muffled sound of someone's heart, presumably mine. But what I'm now getting into is the awareness that there's a sound missing – the eternal outside sound, the rushing monsoony sound, the hiss and pit of the rain on the tin-roof.

Instead there's a voluble quiet – in our bedroom, in our house, and out in the valley and then reaching away to God knows where.

I'm alive to it, very anxious, very much on edge.

That's when I hear somewhere way down in the valley or from over the hill or from outer space, the wind coming. I feel it as a thrill, probably of horror. Know what, this isn't just a squall on its way inland – it's the storm come back. The Big Storm.

Oh Christ, know what it is? It's that shadowy thing with its face hidden coming to find me in the cupboard. But also it's the wind, the searching electrical wind that has an appointment with me. I hear it come churning towards the house.

It hits the house a tremendous buffet. I hear the door slam, something crash in the kitchen. It's going through the house – beats me how it knows I'm here.

I clench my eyes shut as if clenching my eyes might get me lost. Too late – it's into the cupboard. Has got me by the scruff. And then I feel those damn monkeys going to work on me, the electrics from my feet to my staring topknot. My teeth gravel like a coffee-grinder. All over me the neck-hairs are standing on end.

It's over. I've opened my eyes. The cupboard's been blown open. Out there our bedroom is full of silver light. I'm trying to remember the issue, but for some reason I don't seem in touch with it.

I think: I suppose in that case I might just as well come out of the cupboard.

Then I think: Hey, prepared to come out of the cupboard. That's of course, well it has to be, the breakthrough.

102

I hear the front door and then Fiona down in the hall. I shout: "Is that you?"

Fiona calls "Quickly. There's an amazing sunset. Do hurry."

I shout: "You come and see it from up here. I've got all this to tell you."

"No, you jolly well come down. I'm not strong enough for any more revelations."

She's silent a moment. Then she says: "Hey, what's been going on? Looks like a whirlwind's been through the place. What you been up to?"

I'm about to say: "That's what I was saying – I've got all this to tell you..." when I hear a car draw up in the drive.

For some reason I'm holding my breath.

Fiona calls up: "They've come back. The police."

6
SACRIFICE

103

I'm thinking: Last time I woke up feeling this much in the clear, look what happened.

No but that was different. I'd not then decided freely and of my own volition to make the move out of the cupboard. This is the conclusive breakthrough.

I'm lying there feeling luminous and clear and thinking: Maybe what I now know about Ayah and all that, maybe it's something the world is crying out for. Maybe I should be prepared to change my life. Chuck conservatories and make myself available as a counsellor.

Yes that's it, maybe I'm being called to open a kind of clinic, a sort of holistic retreat centre where people mixed-up by the insane pressure of modern life can come and learn from me how to let the breathing do the breathing.

I can't wait to tell Fiona. We could have one of those hot whirly baths, and a wing for things like colonic irrigation, and a nurse in a starched white dress carrying a clipboard. We could buy a place. With a bank loan we could buy a place like... Besseldon Manor.

Besseldon Manor!

Police!

I've been forgetting yesterday evening – being raided by the police.

So much for feeling in the clear.

104

The Police. Sure enough it's the one with the ginger moustache.

He speaks as if reading from his notebook and someone has told him it's best to follow the words with one finger.

"... investigating a break-in of a serious nature at Besseldon Manor. I have been given to understand..."

I ask him into the kitchen. When he's taken off his hat he's more or less down to size. About Dennis's age.

The property had been entered by the glass doors that open into the new conservatory.

I'm thinking: this could be the moment to turn Caruso in. Breech of Contract. Not to mention my commodities. That's right – much better not to, I mean mention. I'm across a barrel. Which, if Fiona's right, is a powder keg, a barrel of dope.

Instead I say: "I can absolutely vouch for my men. Besides it would be damn silly for one of them..."

The property had been vacated at the time of the felony. But the day previous the lady housekeeper had seen this suspicious...

"Ah that could have been Cornelius. My gold leaf man. It's true, he can look very suspicious, but he's... well, he's reliable. I'd trust him (I must be out of my mind) with the Crown Jewels. What I mean is he's not concerned with conventional profit. He's into gold."

This young officer has the ability to lengthen his neck by as much as an inch. Like an emu.

"Into gold?"

"Yes, but the living gold."

"Would it be proper to ask where this gentleman acquires his gold?"

"No, no," I say airily. "He's after the secret of gold."

The officer looks thoughtful, and purses his lips so that his moustache gives the underside of his nose a brush.

"The secret, eh?"

"Yes," I whisper, "this gold, very important it's all kept secret."

Then thinking this might not be entirely helpful, I add, "Was anything taken?"

"With the owner abroad..."

"You can't mean it. He hasn't, has he, done a runner?"

The officer makes an indelible pencil note of what I've said, and then returns to the script.

"With the owner abroad, the housekeeper is not able to be entirely certain. She thinks there was only the one article."

"Yes?"

"A small ornament. What you would term a boodha."

"Good Lord!"

The officer is watching me as if he's detected a confession. And then he says. "Solid gold."

105

The phone beside the bed gives a little stuttered ring – as if someone's making an off-limits call on the extension downstairs, or the engineer's outside somewhere tinkering with the wires.

I don't give it a thought except I find I'm thinking: That sounds fishy. Maybe it would be sensible to just check on that.

No, not what I expected – far worse.

"... it is here to be noted, that the Sages have called this decomposed product..." See, it's Corny, "... on account of its blackness, the raven's head. Get it?"

I'm about to yell: "No, you get it – you get the hell off my airwaves for a start..." when someone says: "No, I don't get it."

SM. The two of them red-handed, having a talk on my telephone.

Corny says: "Hang on, there's more to it. 'In the same way Christ had no form nor comeliness, was the vilest of all men, (What's he mean, 'In the same way...?' I trust it's not me he's likening to this Christ), full of griefs and sicknesses, (See!) and so despised that men even hid their faces from him. Indeed, it is not unfitly compared with Christ when the putrefied body of the Sun lies dead in the bottom of the phial, until as a result of greater heat, its soul by degrees and little by little descends to it again, and once more infuses the decaying body and preserves it from total destruction.' Now do you get it?"

Silence. I think: She's hung up on him. Good. He'll never see sense till people take a strong line on this drivel. When I hear her say: "Right. I do, I get it. But it's fine for you to talk – you don't have him dropping in out of the blue every five minutes."

See, it is me they're talking about. What a colossal cheek! Right that's it, I'm going to...

Corny says: "Come on, don't let it fash you."

SM says: "What d'you mean 'fash' me? I'm not about to let anything fash me."

"You were breathing heavily – I thought you were getting fashed."

"That wasn't me breathing. That was you breathing."

I put my hand over the mouthpiece.

Both of them say: "Ah, that's better."

Then Corny says: "Someone was listening in. You realize he's put the police onto us. They've probably tapped our lines. Maybe you should give your phone a tug, just pull it out of the wall."

SM says: "I already have."

106

I think: This has gone far enough. I'm going to ring the police. If I don't distance myself from this mob I'll fetch up in jail.

I pick up the receiver and dial 999. The call is answered... by silence. Then a couple of clicks. And the other imperious silence which always precedes the answerphone's message.

"This is a recorded message..."

I don't believe it.

"We are, you see decided solitaries." Corny's whisper is serene and urgently confidential. "Each is his own laboratory, and working there for himself experiences intense loneliness. And yet the records of all of us show remarkable agreement on first principles, even if we don't understand what it is we're agreeing about. The knowledge we acquire may not be passed to others unless they are worthy of it. Since all the essentials are expressed in metaphors they can be communicated only to those who possess the gift of comprehension. All are agreed that their art is sacred and divine, and that the opus can be completed only with the help of God. The foolish allow themselves..."

I put the phone down. I've heard all I need to hear. Nothing for it – soon as I'm up I'm going to drive over and confront Corny. Once and for all.

Even if it means... Christ!

107

On my way to the bathroom I bump into Annabel.

She says: "Is it okay with you if I move in with Rex?"

"I beg your pardon?"

"Rex."

"The one you met in the dinner queue?"

"No dad – Rex. Rex is who I've been trying to tell you about."

If she's going to get worked-up, I'm going to get worked-up.

"No, it's certainly not okay with me. That's it. That's final."

"Fine. I was just wanting to know whether I move in with or without your permission."

"Hang on. Where are you rushing off to? What's your mother say?"

"Mum said to ask you."

"Then that settles it. What I mean is, I haven't met Rex have I? Well, have I? There you are. So why not ask him round for supper?"

"I have. Tomorrow. Of course it would help if you could try to act normal."

I think: What the hell do you mean, normal?

Come to think of it what the hell does she mean?

108

I know what she meant. I've cut myself shaving. Twice. My hand is shaking. Well I am, I'm badly shaken.

I walk into the kitchen with my chin tufted with cotton-wool.

I say: "What you looking at me for?"

Fiona is smiling. She says: "Just looking. I was interested to see where, as Annabel would say, you're at this morning. You poor love."

I think: What I'd really like to do is go and sit on Fiona's lap.

I say: "Love, you do understand don't you. I think I'm almost there, back to normal – only more so. In fact I'm pretty sure I'm on the point of a real breakthrough."

And then I'm thinking: Breakdown more likely. Caruso hasn't paid up. The bank manager, I'll probably hear from him today. I've got myself involved with a load of crooks. And now the police have caught up with me. Back to normal? You're out of your mind!

That's when I notice Fiona looking at me. Smiling. But at the same time there are a couple of liquid moonstones, pinky-blue and smokey, one on either cheek. She just nods.

I feel a scalding tremulous pain leap like a spark between the most unlikely points in my body. And then I'm gone.

When I come round I realize that, no, this probably hadn't been a heart attack. Just a momentary vision. In which for a dreaming eternity I'd been an abiding blue deity. Vast, handsome, sublime. Except come to think of it I hadn't actually been him – what I'd been was sitting on his lap. And it was somehow as if I was completely open and able to experience the vast glowing emptiness of his dream. Just momentarily.

But now all that is gone, and I'm left with just the outline of him, like a blue stain somewhere inside between my eyes.

I gasp.

Fiona says: "What's up, what's the matter?"

I say: "It's the breakthrough."

"What, another breakthrough?"

"No, another sort of breakthrough. I just hadn't realized before what it all amounts to."

"What?"

"Come on," I say impatiently, "I mean loving you as much as I do."

Fiona is laughing and wiping her eyes. "Idiot," she says.

I'm beginning to think: A breakthrough is one thing, but maybe this one's going too far. I mean I felt I was practically God or something. That's the big time, and sure as hell I'm not quite ready for that. Too much power – in fact I might already have blown it.

To be honest I feel my fuse has blown. I'm going to have to do something about this urgently. This is something I'm going to have to go into. Or get the hell out of. Before anything else.

Even if it means... Christ!

109

I'm running down the track to SM's cottage. I feel things are coming to an ugly head.

SM and Corny – so what if I have run foul of Bonnie & Clyde Mark II, that's just going to have to be the police's problem. I've got other things on my plate (Viz: God), and there may not be very much time left. I feel there's something dark after me.

No, what I feel is I'm in one of those old dreams and I've got my directions fouled up and I'm actually sprinting towards what I'm running away from. Probably round the next corner I'll run slap into it and that'll be that.

I stop in my tracks. I'm thinking: That wasn't me who screamed. I stand still, hold my breath and try to listen past the pudder in my head. As a matter of fact the whole bleak world is holding its breath. Not a murmur of wind, just the shifty grey listening stillness.

Wait, I think I can hear people in every direction – whistling. Acres away. Eerie, as if from every direction I'm downwind.

Another scream.

I think: That'll be Corny gone berserk. Or perhaps... perhaps they're being raided by the police.

I'm unnerved to find I'm deliberately running on down the track. If I've joined the have-a-go fraternity, there really must have been a breakthrough. Maybe Monty could make a man of me yet. Or God...

110

SM has her palms pressed against her ears while her fingers grope distractedly in her crinkly haywire hair. She's standing outside the cottage door, done up in a black crocheted sweater and a long black skirt. Her face is just the one feature, blank white horror.

She's staring across the yard, out into the meadow.

She screams again: "SHAY-MUS!"

I look where she's looking and think: So that's who that is – Seamus. It's the wolfhound. I thought he'd moved on. The trouble seems to be that he's after a hare. He's going in slow motion, crossing the meadow in about three strides and not bothering to cut corners. The hare is running this way and that – like the clappers.

I say: "I shouldn't worry, he hasn't a hope of catching her."

Which merely provokes SM to scream again.

"SHAY-MUS!"

With that the hare changes tactics, lights off in a straight line for the far end of the meadow. Stops in her tracks. Looks round at Seamus who's trying to bring himself back on line. The hare's running again. Daft, where's she headed? There's a snap and a click. The snap's from the dog's massive mouth and the click is from the hare as, very slowly, frame by frame, it spirals ten feet into the air.

This time when SM screams I think: That's torn it. No one ever heard a scream like it.

With her hands still over her ears she runs into the cottage and slams the door with her foot.

I hear her shouting: "Everything's beastly, I really, really hate everything. And as for you, I hate you."

I'm thinking: This isn't very handy, I'm stuck the same side of the door as Seamus.

111

Finally I decide I'll knock on the door. No reply. I'm wondering what to do when I'm jumped out of my skin by a yell. My yell.

I look over my shoulder. The goat's helping himself to the hem of my jumper. He's looking at me with his superior expression – as if he feels he's seen me somewhere before but can't put a name to the face, as if this yelling were the sort of behaviour he'd expect from me.

I'm thinking: I thought she'd got rid of these animals. She should, she's far too much on her plate.

The door swings open.

"What d'you want this time? Come on for Christsake what do you want?"

Yes, what do I want? I'm trying to think but, what I'm thinking is: What's happened to her eyes? The green's like a shadow. It's as if they'd gone out. And her hair's grey. She's probably been baking, probably got flour in her hair. I'd hardly recognize her.

What's more she can't stand still – looks like she's cracking up and needing the loo at the same time. And the kitchen – what a tip. All that on the floor, I'd rather not guess.

She's regressed into... into rabbits. Under the table, five at least. There in the armchair, poking his head this way and that, like an apoplectic magistrate passing sentence, is the great red-faced muscovy duck.

She says: "God, everything's such a mess."

I think: God, she's right, but how did she guess? Terrible mess.

On the table there's a couple of hive-supers and a pile of honey-frames in a carving dish. The huge barrel-extractor is on its side on the floor in a slow puddle of honey. The place is a siren, full of tetchy bees looking for trouble.

Sounds as if she is beginning to crack: "I should have had this done months ago. Like the honey's gone sugary and stuck in the comb. I tried heating it and (she stops to swallow back her crying) and the wax melted. Everything's in a mess. And now you have to show up."

I say: "At least I'm not the police." Well what she said hurt me, and so this just slips out.

She turns nasty: "Boy-oh, are you going to need the police!" She draws one finger across her throat. Convincingly.

I ignore this. I say meekly: "I felt I was approaching the crisis."

"You'd better believe it."

"I mean the real crisis."

"So?" she says. "Some of us feel it approaching once a month. A regular curse, regular as clockwork. Like with me it's a big issue today. I might have guessed you'd want to get in on it."

Now what on earth's she on about? While I try to figure it I say meekly: "I thought maybe I should get into some work."

"You mean help me with the honey? Too kind."

"I mean, you know, maybe go into it. I mean God or something."

At that she's scared again, looks round nervously as if not sure what she's looking for.

She says: "You'll have to make up your own mind about that. I wouldn't want to be responsible. I've enough on my plate."

"What d'you mean responsible, responsible for what?"

"I don't know what I mean. You brought up the subject. All this picking over the shit, this going into it, yes – sounds creepy to me. You can get stuck in it. It can become a substitute for living. Some people don't ever come out. I wouldn't touch it – it's really dangerous. I mean, like, you never found your wedding ring, did you?"

Looking at her I begin to feel unbearably agitated, the way she's hectically patting her hair with the flat of her hand as if looking for a grip. She stops and closes her dull eyes. Then as she begins to shudder she grabs herself in both arms.

Shuddering, she says: "So why did he have to kill her? Shit, shit."

For a moment I think: Christ, now who's Corny murdered?

Then I think: No of course she means the dog.

She says: "Why can't he just leave me alone? He's forever hassling me. I hate him."

Or does she mean Corny?

I say: "Frankly I think he's off his head. I get just the same, always bugging me on the phone."

"Who?" she says. She's back looking lethal, plenty of lip-curl, not the least upset.

"Sorry, I thought you meant..."

"Go on, you thought I meant?"

"This Corny – he's always on the phone pestering people."

"He's like sick. He scares me shitless." Here we go, she's cracked up again.

I say supportively: "Yes, and he's currently under suspicion of breaking and entering – Caruso's place."

"You're off your nut." She glances over her shoulder, and then says in a whisper, "Him and Caruso – they're like this."

She hooks her two forefingers together and pulls.

I say: "Oh, so you know about Caruso." But what I'm thinking is: Now hang about – it looks like I've stumbled on something big.

And then to give an impression of unruffled normality I say quickly: "What's he say? I mean he's usually blathering on about something."

She's suddenly vague: "Oh he'd picked up about Seamus being about to kill the hare."

I think: Okay, so now which of us is off her nut?

I say: "You don't mean it. What did he say?"

"He said that's fine. The hare represents the material part, or unredeemed instinct which is transformed into spirit by being translated to the moon, from where it shines down upon the earth in the form of divine intuition."

I don't know what to say. What's worse she's started to cry.

"Christ, I hate this shitty business. It's scary. He had no business killing her."

I think: Poor kid, maybe I ought to give her a hug.

She says: "And you keep your filthy hands to yourself. That's all I need. Know something? You're sick. I mean that's what you are, sick."

I say stiffly: "I think there's some misunderstanding. I'll be on my way. Sorry to have bothered you."

There's a whizzing angry noise. I'm hit by fire right between the eyes. I've been stung by a bee.

112

SM wails: "Now look what you've done, you've killed a bee. Christ what's the matter with you?"

I say: "You'll excuse me saying this but it was your bee that chose to sting me, and it's extremely painful."

"You upset him. Bees don't sting for kicks. When a bee stings he stings with the whole of himself. It's a big sacrifice. Stinging kills him, and his insides come out. Oh shit, it's all horrible."

"He should have thought about that before he flew off the handle. You can't pin this one on me." Well I am, I'm in a lot of pain and it's making me irritable.

She hisses: "You upset him. Your energy must be terrible. I've always known you were sick. You ought to do something about it."

I'm thinking: I really could, I could hit her.

Under the table the hound lifts it's head and snarls open four inches of fang. I don't know how he got there. I thought he was outside enjoying jugged hare.

"See, it's your vibes. Seamus's had about enough of you too. I daresay in a minute he's going to bite you. You really did ought to do something about yourself."

Calm and icy I say: "Thank you. That, if you remember, was why I came in the first place. But there's obviously been some misunderstanding. If I can get out of the door in one piece I'll intrude on you no longer."

"Please yourself. But I'd have thought you needed desperately to do some work on yourself. But you please yourself. I don't give a shit. You know where the mattress is. Oh God, what a mess."

SM says: "Just one lousy mess."

She's been cranking the extractor till bits of wax have been flying out and sticking in her hair. She looks if anything, in a worse frame of mind. Her eyes are spiked with tears.

I'd say she looked positively homicidal.

She says: "Christ, you really know how to make a meal of it."

It's true, for some time now I have been having a good cry.

I snivel: "I'm feeling just fi-fi-fine."

She looks at me in an oddly menacing way and says: "Don Juan says, 'Beware of those who weep with realization, for they have realized nothing.'"

I say: "Who's Don Juan?"

"Who's Don Juan? You can't like mean who's Don Juan. Don Juan's Don Juan."

Suddenly the pain from the bee sting between my eyes is unbearable.

I say: "Anyway I hadn't realized I had realized anything."

"That's what I figured. But you're going to have to realize something quick, because you haven't that much time."

"Before what?" I didn't mean to croak.

She looks around the room as if she's heard footsteps, and then looks back at me.

She hisses urgently: "Now listen carefully. This is something you're going to have to catch up with. There's killing and there's killing. Take Seamus. He may not have killed the hare the way you thought. Kill something you're afraid of and what you're trying to do is get shot of it. It doesn't work. All you've done is push it underground. There it is hanging around in the shadows. It's still alive. It's spooking you. But Seamus knows, if you want to get shot of something there's only one way to kill it. You get to know it. You gobble it up. You know it then because it's part of you."

I say: "Well you would, wouldn't you?" I'm not about to disagree with her, not when she's in this mood.

She puts her finger to her lips, glances nervously over her shoulder, and then whispers: "That's right. Know a thing and you become one with it. It no longer has a life of its own. See, you've taken its life. So you've killed it, right? Like when you meet the Buddha, or when you and she's on the job. I mean the real thing, like when she's her experience of you knowing her. You've killed each other. Like it was with Seamus. Poor old, Seamus, done by the hare, Got it?"

I nod enthusiastically because that seems the sensible thing to do. But absolutely no way do I get it. In fact the whole idea seems to be making me quite weepy again. Or else it's the bee sting that's burning and throbbing like crazy.

114

"So what I'm saying is, you kill her."

There's a sort of squeak. That's me saying: "No!"

"Go on kill her. If you don't bring it off this time you've had it."

"No."

"What's her name?"

"Whose name?"

"Whoever it is who's scaring you to death. Your wife or whoever."

"Fiona? I'm not scared of Fiona."

"That's it, Fiona. You kill her."

"No. Absolutely not."

"Why're you keeping your hand clenched?"

"It is, is it? I mean clenched?"

"Sure it's clenched."

"I didn't know it was clenched."

"Maybe it wants to kill her."

"No."

"Maybe you just won't let it do what it wants."

"No I won't."

Now why's she laughing? Her eyes are dangerous, a kind of plutonium green.

She says quietly: "So you go into your hand, go into the clench. Go on face it. How can you be sure you don't want to kill her if you're too chicken to see whether that's not what your hand's itching to do?"

115

My hand grip is terrific, clenched and set, ready for violence. I give a hell of a snarl. That's not a good idea. I seem to have excited Seamus. He comes stalking over with a kind of open-minded expression, climbs on the mattress and puts his leg over me. It's not unlike being mounted by a giraffe.

SM says: "He seems to think you're worth knowing. That's why he's about to kill you."

116

SM says: "That's enough of that Seamus, you never did know when to stop."

117

The room's silent, like a zoo after the three-minute warning. The rabbits' eyes are popping out of their heads. SM has her hands over her ears. Seamus has got his shock on end and is squinting in a fixed way as if he'd a hornet on the end of his nose.

The silence that follows my scream is utterly empty. I take a look inside – nothing.

An emphatic nothing. I'm packed out with it, full to the brim with an unbelievable emptiness. What's more I've unclenched my fist.

SM says: "You realize you were crazy to let her off the hook."

She's been yanking the extractor. She's panting. She looks hot, haywire and evil.

I say, dryly: "So what do you suggest I do?"

She turns and stares at me.

Then she's walked across the room and is standing at the head of the mattress. Just behind where my head is, looking down at me and offering me this murderous great kitchen knife.

I say: "Uh-uh not that, no way."

She gives the knife a good shake, insistent I take it.

I say: "No."

My body has begun to twist this way and that in some sort of torment. At the same time the bee sting's burning a kind of white black-out between my eyes.

"See, you don't have the spunk to make it, do you? You want the hell out of it. All you want's the quick black-out."

I stop moving and look up at her. The room's gone still again.

She's looking down at me. I realize that her green, ravenous gaze is on top of me. It's covering me like a bell-jar.

Now what's she doing? She's lifted the front of her black skirt off the ground, about nine inches, gathered it up slowly with her fingers.

She moves so quickly I can't tell for sure what's happened. She's lifted the skirt over my head. The hem's across my throat. I think she must have kneeled down, her knees either side of my head, and kneeling on the hem so that my head's inside and the hem's tight across my neck.

And she's still on about something. Only I'm too tied up to listen. She gives the hem a yank.

"Will you kindly listen!" she says. Anyone can tell she's laughing. Except she isn't, she's crying. Terrible state.

Okay, I'm listening.

She's saying: "You never see anything, do you! I can't see you any more.

Not ever. I shouldn't have let myself get involved... it's most unprofessional. Start fancying a client, there's shit everywhere."

The last I remember is struggling to extricate myself. But I wouldn't say I was being very effective. I wouldn't even say I was trying very hard.

119

I'm lying on the mattress feeling terrible. I feel exhausted. I feel all roughed-up and foul.

I realize I've of course let everybody down. What I've done or what I've been party to or just been prepared to go along with, is quite inexcusable. I very much doubt whether anyone is ever going to speak to me again.

The room is remarkably unimpressed. SM's over at the table. She's putting tops and labels on a row of full honey-jars. All the animals look hypnotised, in particular the goat and rabbits who squint as they continue to chew.

SM licks a label and says: "Now try saying there wasn't a crime. This time you've really done it."

I nod energetically. Well I do I want to make a clean breast of it. But what the hell is it I've done? I must have allowed myself to be carried away.

I say: "What happened? I mean what did I do?"

"You trying to say you don't remember?"

"I don't."

"Like you don't want to face it."

"I do. Except I don't know if I do because I don't know what I did. What did I do?"

"You finally brought it off."

"You don't mean it! I feel something that could be a memory beginning to stir. I think I feel better. In fact I'm not sure I don't feel a bit of a dog.

"Yes you finally went through with it."

"Mumma!"

"You can say that again!"

I ignore this and say: "So what did I do?"

"I told you, you brought it off."

I groan: "Will you please tell me what did I do?"

She doesn't look up. In fact for a minute she doesn't do anything. Then with a jerk of her thumb she points over her shoulder.

120

But I'm already out of the door.

I can hear SM back in the cottage yelling: "Who was it said no one had committed a crime? Police! POLICE!"

Her laughter comes running after me like a mad rooster.

The entire landscape's whistling again... Police whistles. At the same time there's a helluva commotion in the house as if the animals are scrapping to be first after me out of the door.

I'm sprinting up the track. Something's after me. Probably some goat. Probably it's Seamus.

I stop and look back. No there isn't anything. In fact not only does the world seem suddenly to have settled down, but the place looks oddly deserted.

I think: This is unreal – why should I be feeling in the clear? Maybe I ought to go back. Then I think: What's there to go back for? You saw it. That was enough.

And I did see it, I still can. I saw her over there, mountainous on the sofa, being run upon by a couple of rabbits: that fat slob Ayah with the kitchen knife stuck in her back.

I continue up the track, but then stop again and put my finger to the blazing bump on my forehead. I look at the finger as one would to see if it's wet.

There it is on the fingertip, the tiny black needle, the bee sting.

7
YEAST

121

I'm back in the quadrangle. In the far corner, with a gang of rugby rowdies, is Telfont. They're dragging some unfortunate diminutive Bernard Levin-like person towards the Fellows' Garden, presumably to give him the fishpond treatment.

I seem to have got myself elected president of the Students' Union, which is why when Telfont gives me a leer I think: I really ought to be putting a stop to that sort of behaviour.

The previous head of the Students' Union appears and says: "Aren't you coming to the ceremony, it's the one really important thing that happens in this place."

I say: "Yes of course but first I must put on a tie."

I run to my room at the top of the tower. So this time it's my tie I'm not able to find.

But what I do find is... there's something in my bed. At which moment the bedclothes fall back and there is a beautiful young waking Fiona, naked and... and unbelievable. It's as if my life has broken into the place.

We talk and she says she's prepared to make a life with me.

It's then I feel I have to come clean. The infernal exam: Ancient History – I haven't done the work and I've now left it too late. Which means I won't get a degree, which means I won't ever have a job, which means...

Though at the same time I'm thinking: Actually I'm not sure I have left it too late. In fact now I think about it, maybe I have done the work. Fiona looks evasive.

At that moment, beyond my door, which is so battered and ill-fitting I can see everything through the cracks, a long procession of exalted, rather reverential people is making its way up the tower-stairs – to sing the May-morning anthems on the roof.

Fiona says: "Why do you always have to wake me? I was having a dream. You and me's..."

"Wait, wait! Now you're awake you've got to let me tell you mine or I'll forget it. I was in..."

"Will you be quiet! I'm beginning to forget. You and me's..."

"Listen, I've been awake hours waiting to tell you mine..."

There's a bang on the door.

"Now then you two what's going on? Not that I want to know." It's Annabel.

Fiona and I shout: "He (she) won't shut up and let me tell my dream. Now I'll forget."

"You two must find each other really really fascinating. Anyway don't forget – we've got Rex coming to dinner."

I say: "Rex!"

"Yes daddy, Rex. Remember?"

I say: "That's it, REX, I do remember."

What I'm remembering is this other dream: A still October evening by the wood-fringed lake. Almost certainly going to freeze. New moon. Magpie in the ash tree. The lake black and oily and full of stars. Corny (or could it be Caruso?) is out in the middle, splashing about, a last desperate effort to swim. His voice wavers over the water, doleful and resigned: *"Rex mortus est."*

I say: "That's it I must check on Corny. I've heard he and Caruso are definitely in cahoots. I'll give him a ring and come straight to the point."

Fiona says: "Not till you've heard my dream you don't."

"Quick then."

"You and me's in this double bed..."

"Good."

"What you mean good?"

"Well don't you think that's good?"

"Just listen. Lying on the foot of the bed is this distressed woman.

Between her and us, sitting up and facing me, is a baby, the most beautiful dark-haired little girl about 18 months old, smiling and happy and looking at me so loving and oh, gentle and..."

"Yes, yes get on with it."

"I say to you 'How's that for a baby then?' That's when the woman speaks. She looks desperate. She says they've come and slept in our bed because they've nowhere else to go."

Fiona's sitting up, hugging her knees and looking at me rather shyly. Beautiful.

I say: "Did you dream that?"

She nods.

I say: "Beautiful. That has to be a really beautiful dream."

We look at each other for a time, and then I say: "But now I'd better go and give Corny a buzz."

123

Orders. I'm in the office thinking how I'll put it to Corny, when I think: First I may as well check the answerphone.

There's a call: Mrs Pritchard, acquainted with Besseldon Manor, would like to discuss an extensive conservatory.

She means Embezzlement Manor; she means the Great Caruso! I'll be requiring a fat non-commodity-based deposit from her. But this is something to tell the bank manager.

Wait! There's another call: Lady Vine has admired the new conservatory at Besseldon Manor and would like a quotation. To include gold leaf of course.

Can this be for real? Something about it I don't like. It's the Caruso connection. I could be on my way to the cleaners. Maybe this is something else I should check out with Corny.

I dial his number – and get this kind of stuck in the groove burr. I try again. Same thing. I ring the operator and have her try. "Line discontinued," she says.

"I beg your pardon?"

"Discontinued. That number's been discontinued quite some time."

124

Sheet rain. I'm driving round to Corny's place. I'm going to check him out once and for all.

I think: No, this is daft. If his number's discontinued I'm wasting my time. First I should check this out with SM. Check out just what exactly those two interlocking fingers of hers were saying about Corny and Caruso.

Wait a minute! I mean, after what happened last time. I might as well go home and turn on an electric chair

125

I run down the track, entirely open to the slow murderous rain. When I reach the cottage I'm wet as a fish. I knock. Not a dickey-bird. I knock again harder. This time the door breathes open.

The place is empty. Not entirely empty, but it feels empty. But not entirely empty. The kitchen table's still there. No chairs. In fact nothing else except laid out neat on the floor, the mattress.

I think: She can't be gone long because the place still feels warm. In fact I'd guess the Rayburn is still alight.

I don't feel entirely at ease with the silence – it's like the silence when somebody's hiding and biting her lower lip so as not to laugh.

I think: She's fooling again. They're probably upstairs together waiting to see what I get up to.

But at the same time I know perfectly well this isn't so – I know she's gone.

There's a mug on the table and beside it a piece of paper. The mug's still hot and is full of some herby sort of drink. The paper is a note which says: *Help Yourself.*

I take off my sodden jacket and hang it on the Rayburn rail. After thinking about it seriously for a bit I decide I'll also take off my trousers. Then I start drinking the mug of herb tea. I think: Mmmm, Red Zinger. But I know I'm fooling myself. It isn't Red Zinger, it's got an odd fiery coconutty tang with several inflammatory after-flavours.

Nowhere to sit so I lie down on the mattress. This situation is mystifying. It is on the face of it quite probably tragic. I suggest to myself that I should be feeling outraged, or let down, or worried sick, or bereft, or plain sad – but I can't get in touch with any of these feelings. I just go on sipping the drink and feeling increasingly unfeeling.

I try to imagine what SM would say, and I hear her say: "So you go into the non-feeling – finally that's where it's at."

I smile and think: Alright, here goes.

126

The pain is indescribable. I've just come from being with my girlfriend. She's grown a good deal. She's pregnant – oh so beautiful. But she's harrowed. She's afraid she's losing the baby. Obviously at the time I had to appear positive, but now I can't help crying with compassion and grief and helplessness.

Just as the pain is becoming insupportable I have what seems like a revelation that the pain isn't some vague thing I'm feeling for her – it's a very definite thing she's doing to me. My girlfriend... I don't believe it. She's got this grip on me, and the grip is tightening all the time.

I'd prefer not to describe what happens next... except if this isn't important then I can't imagine how anything else could ever be important.

There's this thing over my head feels like a pouch of tripe with a hell of a grip. But what it is, so help me... it's her great muscular vulva that's clamped itself down over my head and shoulders. I'm wriggling, tossing... everything I know to get free, but I'm not going to make it.

I say: "Let her go!"

I'm thinking: Let her go, that's an odd thing to say. But she does, she weakens.

I say it again: "Let her go!" She is, she's weakening. "Let her go!"

The grip eases from my neck, and is slipping from my head.

"Let her go!" She's letting go.

She's let go. Someone's thwacked me on the bum. I've begun to breathe.

127

I'm kneeling there on the mattress experiencing the emptiness of the room. The emptiness seems to carry some delicious meaning.

I say: "The house is empty." I feel I've said something enormously profound.

I'm looking around, vaguely aware there may be a detail I've overlooked. My hand contacts me. I look down at it. Why... my fingers are clenched again. Around... oh no, not that again... around the handle of SM's kitchen knife. It's too boring. There must be better things to do with the rest of my life than to keep on stabbing old Ayah in the back.

I think: Okay, so I'll just let it drop. But the message doesn't get through to my fingers.

I intend to say: "But look I've forgiven her." But what I hear is a voice saying: "Be a man."

I wouldn't have thought it was my voice.

I can feel the violence coming back.

I intend to say: "But there wasn't a crime, remember?"

But what this voice says is: "Be a man."

The violence is coming for me.

I try to say: "But we've been through all this before." But the voice says: "Yes but that time you didn't know you'd done it. Not till afterwards. That's not good enough."

I say: "Look at her she's so little she's pathetic."

"Who, Ayah?"

"No."

"Mummy?"

"No, all of them."

"Ah, your girlfriend. So get on with it. Be a man."

Oh God. I've recognised the target. And I know that I need and long to have gone through with it. In the end I do this brilliant thing – I let it happen.

Even where the knife goes home, stabbing again and again as I grunt in horror and choke and sob my relief. I thrust in the knife to the hilt and turn it. This way. That way. This way.

A long time I am kneeling, surveying what I have done, fingering the gouts of horsehair on the rent mattress. I just kneel there exhausted, removed from the column of slow churning horror and relief. I wish I could feel. What I'd like to feel is pity.

At last I lay my head on that torn tender place.

128

The Extraordinary Dance. I'm dancing. It's what I'd describe as a kind of slow ceremonial dance. I'd say it was definitely a temple dance. The style and flavour of it is very much the small ads in the back of *Homespun* magazine. On one leg with my hands making dreamy meanings in the air. I imagine the origins of Tai Chi lie in this sort of dance.

I'd say this was, beyond question, an androgynous sort of dance. I'm flowing to it. I don't feel I'm holding anywhere.

The humming stops. The dancing is over. I look up. I'm impressed to discover my hands in front of my face in prayer posture. I go down on my knees. And then forward and down so that my head rests on the mattress.

The room is full of blue light, and of someone's singing so contented and so dreamy that I can't quite hear it.

Maybe there isn't singing – but this clear feeling I have is the feeling I'd be getting if I were listening to a woman's contented dreamy singing. A woman I was particularly fond of. In fact very probably a woman I loved. The light is bright which makes every object seem shadowy and translucent.

I think it must be SM singing.

I think: That must be her, a violet shadow over by the window moving to and fro. What on earth's she doing that's making her so content.

I see, she's making bread. She's kneading the dough, with the ball of her fist, pressing down from the shoulder. I can see that from her outline. She fetches more flour and sprinkles the board and then she's kneading again.

And all the time she kneads the bread she is I know, even though I can't quite hear it, singing...

129

SM's Song. If I go into the feeling that she is singing, then I know what it is she is singing about.

She's singing about the feeling being the feeling. How if one stays with that feeling, which is the unspeakable feeling of the two come together, then there is no longer knowledge of parting or of loss – there is only the eternal discovery of the two being one, the two eternally discovering themselves anew in the feeling of being one, eternally rediscovering the wonder of this togetherness which is the totally unexpected and unforeseen wonder of having this child.

I think: I wouldn't want ever to forget this singing of hers. But there are no words – nothing to remember but the feeling. So I must remember the feeling.

130

I wouldn't like to say for how long I've been watching SM making the bread and singing about all this, but clearly she's now finished. She's walking across the room. I can see her against the light, as if she had emerged out from the mist of blue light.

I'd like to call to her, say how much I've been with her singing, but I don't know that that would be possible. I'm not sure there would be much correspondence between my voice and where her singing is. I can't be sure she even knows I'm here.

As she walks across the room towards the door to the stairs she doesn't look at me. The green of her dress is iridescent, but at the same time she is walking in her own shadow, she is silhouetted by shadow, which is softly outlined by the blue light.

"Wait!"

I sit up suddenly, startled by my own exclamation. The room is empty. SM has presumably gone upstairs.

I think: To think I've been coming all these months and have never suspected. You'd think I'd have noticed. I mean you don't get to be this pregnant overnight.

Not this beautifully unmistakably pregnant.

131

Eau de Vie. I'm lying down. I'm thinking: I wouldn't like to have to describe how I'm feeling.

I'm feeling wide open like a sheet of water, but not empty water, water full up with the reflection of the sky – no not the sky but something more centred: the sun, the fiery sun, except in this water the sun is everywhere, by which I mean its centredness is everywhere.

That's what I am – everywhere clear and cool and enflamed.

I'm like an expanse of liquid fire, in fact that's what I feel like.

Firewater – a complete shot of eau de vie.

132

I'm lying there when I hear a sound on the stairs. I experience an expectant stirring all through me of liquid fiery affection. I can't describe how tenderly excited I now am to see SM.

The door at the front of the stair opens. Because the skirt of her pale dawn-blue sari is tight she steps sideways from the bottom stair into the room.

An Indian girl. Her long hair is liquid black, gleaming with a kind of laughter. Her fullness, her joy is so immense she cannot begin to contain it – her brown face so luminous and content beyond any expression she appears almost impassive.

She's walking (though walking's never a word to describe the glide of an Indian girl in a blue sari) slowly across the room towards the front door.

Whether or not I'm dreaming, she's in a dream.

She is definitely going to meet her lover. She has paused, wondering is there something she's forgotten?

Just a moment in passing her eyes' dark question lights on me. For a part of that moment I am everything that is broadcast in her expression – this stillness, the deep, the infinite dark openness upon which a smile is implied.

I feel a sudden emptying – a delicious fullness of that emptiness one experiences when a pain, accepted so long it had become unnoticeable, is removed.

I hear the front door close softly. The light in the room dims as the curtains drift back into place.

I'm listening to the monsoon heaviness of the rain.

I breathe a vestige of light, something no sense can cling to – a delicious fragrance of cardamom.

133

So that's it. I leave the rent mattress on the floor, but return the knife and the mug to the kitchen table. There's a jar of honey which I hadn't noticed earlier.

I'm about to make for the door when I again catch sight of SM's note. *Help Yourself* is crossed out. Something's been added. The handwriting is unquestionably SM's – there's the little o-dot to the i. I look around the room, but no, the mystery is written too deep.

I glance again at the note: *The honey is for you and don't forget to take your bread out of the oven.*

I hold the honey up to the dim winter light. It glows like a jar of translucent gold. I go, for some reason on tiptoe, over to the Rayburn.

It is still warm. I open the top oven. There, brown and cooked to perfection, is a small round cottage loaf.

134

Fiona and I decided it would be more informal to eat in the kitchen.

A mistake. Rex, all grey serge six-foot-double-breasted-four of him, is held together by the kind of straight lace that needs a lord mayor's banquet-hall if it's not to choke itself to death.

Not for him our new authentic smokey oil-lamp, the red-handled cutlery and the chipped French-style white Habitat soup-bowls.

I'm thinking: Clearly what's dazzled Annabel is Rex's style. Must need a hefty annuity to keep him in haircuts. Haircuts and serge – it's all stuff I've been through in my time, but I suppose she's new to it.

Well she's just going to have to find out for herself – I'm not about to influence her one way or the other. I wish though he didn't remind me quite so much of Telfont.

I say: "When I was at college I had a friend called Telfont who used to throw people in the Fellows' fishpond."

I hadn't intended this to sound like an accusation so I add quickly: "Actually I can't say he was really a friend."

Annabel says: "Can I pour Rex some wine?"

I say: "Like wine do you Rex? Yes, of course you may, please. That was another thing about Telfont, terror for drink. And women."

Rex holds out his glass and says: "Just a small one." He breathes out through his nose ingratiatingly and looks to Fiona for approval.

I glance at Annabel. First time I ever saw her drink soup out of the side of her spoon. You'd expect Rex to drink soup out of the side of his spoon. At least he manages not to slurp like Dennis.

I say: "Well Rex, how's tricks in Upper Yuppiedom?"

Annabel says: "Daddy, please!"

Fiona says: "No, but you can see what your father means – lovely suit."

I say quickly: "That's what I meant, smart suit. Anyway what are you into Rex?"

Rex swallows his wine as if it's full of lumps. He says: "I'm training to be a, you know, quantity surveyor."

I'm thinking: He may know how to handle his soup, but he's poor on conversation. Quantity surveyor. How about that for a conversation stopper.

I say: "Big?"

"Excuse me?"

"The quantities."

"Daddy, for God's sake!"

I say: "We'd better have some more wine."

Rex says: "Well just a small one."

Fiona says: "I think there's someone at the door."

I say: "That'll be Dennis."

Fiona says: "Dennis, why should it be Dennis?"

I say: "I was just thinking about him, the way he slurps his soup. What's called a weird coincidence."

Annabel says: "Rex doesn't slurp his soup."

I say: "Well done. Give him some more wine."

Rex says: "No thanks, well maybe just a... thanks."

Fiona says: "I'll see who it is."

I say: "No you don't, I'll go."

It is, it's Dennis. Dennis and a rather beautiful girl. Good grief it's Jennie. I never thought I'd be pleased to see Dennis. And/or Jennie.

I say: "Come on in, you're just in time."

"For what?"

"You'll see."

135

Rex stands up and shakes Dennis's hand. Dennis grimaces and is left massaging his elbow.

Fiona says: "My, don't you both look well."

It's true. Even if Jennie does still have a ball of Kleenex tissues tucked in the sleeve of her jumper, they look relatively unused. Her jumper! Yes she is, she's wearing a V-necked jumper. And jeans. Tight jeans.

"Dad!"

"What d'you mean, dad?"

"Do you have to gape?"

Alright, but you should see the way Jennie's gazing at Dennis. She looks positively... well dangerous. She whispers to Dennis: "You tell."

"No you."

Something's happened to Dennis too. The good-looking bit, it's somehow come to the fore. I now see what they meant about him looking like me. Jennie gives Fiona an unctuous glance, then turns to me.

She says: "We did like you said."

"You did! You didn't did you? What did you do?"

"We've been on that weekend."

"Not..."

"That's it. African Dance as an Energetic Experience." The table is silent. Not, though, a uniform silence. For instance, Rex's silence is the wide-eyed sort, Annabel's the narrow-eyed.

I say: "Excellent. You have Annabel to thank, it was advertised in the back of her magazine."

Annabel says: "Oh that magazine, I don't take that any more."

Fiona says: "Oooo lovely, what did you get up to?"

"You tell."

"No you."

"No go on, you."

Dennis gathers himself. Not even Rex can be unaware that the silence is braced for revelation.

Dennis says: "She encountered her primitive soul."

"Oh shit!"

"Annabel, please!"

Jennie says: "No that's right – it was really, really wonderful."

I'm feeling a funny buzzing feeling in my bee sting.

"So what was it like, this primitive soul?"

"You tell."

"No you, go on you show them."

I glance round. Rex is in trouble. He's got his chin pulled in parade-ground fashion, so far I think it's interfering with his windpipe. He's sweating heavily. Annabel with eyes black as cordite is holding me responsible. Fiona's blue-eyed and already dabbing at her cheeks with her napkin because she's so happy. And hot. And Dennis, eyes shut, head swaying, has started to knock up a heart-of-darkness bongo rhythm on his thighs.

Jennie gets ominously to her feet. Her eyes, vacant as mother night, are beginning to roll. She's raising her hands above her head. The demon rhythm is after her. She's cast Tipp-ex to the wind and has – hips, thighs, unimpeded breasts – begun to dance. A shuffling one-woman fertility dance that involves a complete circuit of the table.

The whirring in my bee sting is reaching critical pitch. I think: What was that? That was like somebody's foot on my foot. I look round. Fiona. She's looking at me that special way, that misty, blue-eyed way...

I see a flash. It's as if the bee sting has cracked open. For a second I'm listening to a screeching static sound. And then out of me, as if I'm an old tanoy, above the howl-back, this dry unmistakable voice: "Let us give full-hearted thanks that Ayah and her Ethiopian now are wed."

I manage to breathe: "Dammit it's Corny." Before my head hits the table.

136

I open my eyes. Not surprising I've been feeling so comfortable – my head's in Fiona's lap. I'm looking into her face.

She says: "You alright?"

"Yes, I'm fine."

I see she's unbuttoned her blouse.

"You alright?"

"I'm fine. I got hot."

"Where've they gone?"

"I thought it was time they went."

"Oh."

I feel very comfortable. Everything's in order.

I say: "It's like meditation – finally you give up. The mind's played its last trick, and you've let it go. You've let go – even of the need to let go. You're completely empty. Empty and complete. Know what I mean?"

After a time Fiona makes the smallest movement with her head.

I say: "Maybe that's why I needed to lose my ring."

Fiona gives her little between-the-eyes questioning frown.

"I had to learn to let go. We're not free if we're not free of each other."

Suddenly I close my eyes tight. I've had a heavy feeling, as if the enormity of the future is standing over our house.

I say: "Fiona, I don't want to be free of you, not ever, ever, ever."

"Perhaps you have to be free before you can choose freely not to be free."

After a while I sigh and open my eyes. She's looking down at me. I think: She doesn't look old, I can't say she looks any age. It's that expression again – the smile, and her eyes brimming.

I say: "Yes, yes you're right. When you're free you've nothing to lose."

Fiona says: "Love, I've been thinking – perhaps now Annabel's almost grown-up... maybe you'd like me to take over the business?"

I look at her, and then I say: "What gave you that idea?"

"I don't know really. I've been taking this evening class in business management..."

"Why didn't you tell me?"

"I didn't like to. I felt perhaps you'd feel..."

"But you know all about business management."

"That's why I was taking the course. I was teaching it."

"So that's what you've been doing."

"Wednesday evenings. Somehow you were never around and..."

"I thought you were out with, with..."

"I was. He's one of my students. Anyway what I thought was, if I did that then you'd be free to..."

I think: Christ, now what's she trying to tell me?

I don't say anything for a time, then I say: "You mean... I'd be free to write my wonderful best-selling book?"

"Yes."

I say: "How's this for a title, Robinson Caruso ?"

8

CONIUNCTIO

or

THE MYSTERIOUS MARRIAGE

137

Christmas Morning. I've woken and it's still dark. I have a feeling it's summer. But also I can feel a weight on my feet which I know is my stocking.

Fiona and Annabel haven't forgotten. Good. We must all have our stockings. I think: I bet right at the bottom, right in the toe, there's a tangerine.

But that doesn't stop me feeling it's summer – about three in the afternoon, the house empty, all the windows open, the doors too, and the air like blue light drifting through, the curtains moving in and out dreamily as the house breathes. The house empty, the house full, the doors open, she everywhere.

I sit up – I've had a very bad dream. I've dreamed that someone has told me in confidence that Corny is President Clinton's son.

I think: Come on, that's not such a bad dream. And I lie down again.

138

Annabel is waking me. She's saying: "Can't think why Santa bothers with someone who's not interested in stockings."

I say: "Me! Not interested in stockings! I'll have you know... wait. I'm remembering a dream."

"Dad-EEE, please, it's Christmas. Stuff the dreams."

"No hang on, I dreamt I had this present from Corny. A picture, a child's head. He said it's very precious, the centre part of a triptych. And here's me not having given Corny so much as a thought."

What I'm thinking is: He may be off his head and a crook, but it is Christmas and we're told Christ does come in the most unlikely guises and he did do this work for me. I haven't even sent him a card. I'm going to have to dash over with something. I know, I'll tell him about President Clinton... and I can check him out at the same time.

I say: "You two stuff the goose. I just need to pop out and see a man about some seasonal commodities."

<h1 style="text-align:center">139</h1>

I turn off the main road – half a mile in sunlight, past the farm with the green silo, over the little stone bridge, and it's the first track on the left. Corny's place.

Soon as I see it I know he's flown. The inside-out stable has a winter-deserted look, as if the wind has been through it.

I draw up in the mud beside the sump of the old rusted generator. Get out and stand a moment surveying the scrap, the brilliant frost, the arctic clear sky, and listening to the bells from the distant parishes that sound somehow brilliant and frosty and gift-wrapped.

I'm thinking: He's not here, but maybe I should just check. When I see there's a piece of paper tacked to one of the huge black double-doors. A piece of card in fact. When I take hold of a corner the tack comes away.

The ink looks new. I read: *Help Yourself.*

Help Yourself – I'm wondering what to think about this when in a low-key investigative way I turn the card over. On the back, written small and neat in Indian ink, what looks like a poem. It's titled... you're not going to believe this, it's titled: *SM.*

> *At the outset*
> *It is a moment too soon*
> *One could not say anything for certain*
> *She has her finger to her lips*
> *The sign of caution*
>
> *When the work is under way*
> *One cannot risk saying a word*
> *The least distraction and the moment might be missed*

She has her finger to her lips
The sign of concentration

At the conclusion
It is already too late
The moment can never be repeated
She has her finger to her lips
The sign of the secret.

I've read all this, and am thinking: Most unusual, but what do I do now, do I go in? When I hear not even the engine, just the tyre-stealth of a car on the track.

I look round with the self-incriminatingly effusive welcome of the red-handed. Wait a minute, it's...

It's the police.

First to climb from the car is the young one with the ginger moustache.

I say: "Good morning, officer. A happy Christmas to you."

He's brought his boss with him – a gigantic man who seems to have chosen his uniform in the belief he may still have a good way to grow. One of those senior policemen who nod and hold their hands together behind their back and leave the talking to the other ranks.

"Surprised to see you here sir."

I say: "Yes, weird coincidence. I was just delivering a Christmas card."

The policemen don't move, but something passes between them – like a knowing nod.

I say: "This was on the door." I hand him the poem. He submits it to a quick forensic glance... that goes on for some time.

"SM," he says finally in circumstantial deadpan, and gives me what I would call 'a look'.

"Evidently we're... I mean someone's expected. It says, *Help Yourself.*"

The younger policeman unhooks and lifts open the door.

"After you," he says.

I wouldn't necessarily have chosen to lead the way.

Plenty of evidence that Corny's moved on. The shelves are mostly empty, and the benches and tables clear of all but the empties or the hopelessly rusted or the tins of what's gone hard.

However centre stage, away from any rubbish, is a pile of cartons, new and sealed with that ribbon-metal for whose undoing there's no known method. And a little apart, on a packing case, two more cartons the same.

The policemen wander around with their hands behind their backs, and the marked disinterest of prospectors seriously interested in buying the place. We all know it's the pile of cartons they're making for.

First the two on the packing case.

The ginger moustache looks over at me, and he taps the top of the top carton with his forefinger three times.

I walk over and look where the forefinger is pointing.

I say: "Good Lord, what a coincidence! Well I'm damned."

There, printed on the top, is my name.

I say: "Officer, I can explain everything."

Since no-one else seems about to say anything I say: "What I mean is... it's totally inexplicable."

On balance, I would say I sounded more or less innocent.

"You wouldn't object if we opened this container?"

"No, no. On the contrary. Help yourself."

While the senior officer assesses the ceiling the younger struggles with the metal tie. Finally he comes up with the ways and means – an old chair leg. Then the stapled cardboard, the packing chips and there...

One can tell by the wind-in-the-corn rustle of his moustache that even the law has been subject to a sharp intake of breath. He holds the contents of the carton in the palm of his hand – a small gold Buddha.

The senior officer glances at it, glances at me, and looks back at the ceiling. But I'm not fooled – I know I'd only have to make a dash for it to find his hand on my collar.

I say: "Ah yes, good. That explains it. Commodities."

Which is one better than bursting into tears.

140

I say: "And that's it really."

While I've been unburdening myself the senior officer's kept closing one eye as if maybe he's detected a hole in the roof. His subordinate's been out of his depth – notebook at the ready, constantly licking the point of his pencil, but incapable of committing himself to paper.

He says: "I may have to ask you sir to come into the station and put all you've just said in a statement."

I say: "Any time. Glad to. Absolutely."

"Thank you sir for your help." For some reason he makes this sound like a severe sentence. About fifteen years. In the meantime, I'm free to go.

Even the senior man watches as I drive away.

I'm half up the track, right on the bend, when I'm put almost in the ditch by the sort of large black limousine Al Capone used when he meant business. For heists and a quick get-away, I expect he used a plumber's van. Except that what's clearly criminal in this case is the caution it's being driven with. We manage to inch past each other. Until our driving windows are level...

I'm not about to recognize him. Something not reciprocated. I can see he's electric-buzzing open his window. And with his other hand he's waving. But I've made it – leaving a shower of mud on his boot. It wouldn't help my position to be found conferring with Caruso at this stage in the investigation. Besides if he's got something he needs to unburden he'll find a person (or persons) at the top of the track who'll be prepared to take it down in longhand.

Back on the road I think: Know what I could use? A Red Zinger. Double strength.

I think: After all, criminal if she were there on her own at Christmas. Besides it's not totally inconceivable I'll find it's where Corny has fetched up.

Did I say, criminal? I think I'll rephrase that.

141

Gleaming. The whole world's gleaming. My shoes crunch down the gleaming frosty track. The two magpies keep pace, hopping silently from twig to twig, one to each side of the track, all the way to the yard.

I can't believe what's happened to the cottage. A hole in the roof right above the bedroom, with the slates dipping in. Several window panes are blown. The kitchen window's off its hinges, and hanging over the sill a sodden tattered old mattress leaking horsehair.

The kitchen door is toppled half-open. The screws in the bottom hinge have dragged from the rotten wood. I lift it out of the mat-well, dragging the remnants of the sisal mat.

No furniture left, not a stick. Soot dribbles have leaked from the Rayburn. The hotplate is rusted. Two dead starlings among the leaves in the corner. The place smells of death.

I think: That's it. Maybe I had to come though. Maybe I had to have seen it.

I turn to leave when... I stop and am listening. Know something? There's somebody upstairs. I can hear the movement. I think: Good God, it can't be. I think: They are, they're coming down the stairs, treading with care on the rotten sleepers.

She stops still when she sees me. She's perfectly calm though I can see she's been crying.

I say: "Love, it's you, what on earth are you doing here?"

Fiona says: "What do you think I might be doing?"

"Yes, but how...?"

"Ssh! It's finished."

And she puts one finger to her lips.

We look at each other. She keeps her finger to her lips. During this time I know everything and know nothing.

Finally I whisper: "Is anything left up there?"

She shakes her head: "Nothing. The only thing here was this – I found it when I arrived, nailed to the door."

She hands me a piece of card. There it is: *Help Yourself.* But I can't be

sure it's the same writing
I turn the card over. I seem to know what to expect.

A heartbreak song the life in my vein
A baby locked in stone
But I will steal in the deepest mine
Rubies from the moon

But I will steal in the deepest mine
Rubies locked in stone
A heartbreak song the life in my vein
A baby from the moon.

It's then I remember the feeling. That last line, when she was singing and I couldn't hear any words.
Well now I know – these were the words. The feeling, the poem. The child.

142

I look up at Fiona and after some time I say: "You know I do, I feel I've completed something. Something huge, only bigger, more like cosmic, and at the same time absolutely imperceptible and of no conceivable interest to anyone. I'm wondering where I've been these last months. Was any of it real? I've been totally unhinged. Potty. Preposterous. God knows what you and Annabel made of it. But I seem finally to have collided with and broken my head against some outcrop of sanity. Yes, that's it. Previously sanity was a way of existing without feeling the pain. The new sanity is existing with what's left when the pain's been felt for what it is – in other words a way of feeling in the clear."
I'm listening to all this, and thinking: Well, what do you know!
In a voice not wholly her own, Fiona says: "Ah, so the feeling is the feeling. Right?" She smiles.

Is she teasing? I'm not sure.

"Right," I say. And then I say, "And all those other feelings, fear and lust and jealousy and so on, they're simply ways of feeling the feeling – fearful or lustful or jealous ways. But what they feel, I mean the feeling, the feeling is... well, of course it is, isn't it, it's... well lets face it, it's... love."

Right.

143

From the door I look back, the last look. I feel I'd like to be feeling something. Anything.

Fiona's waiting in the yard, stamping her feet, upping her shoulders to get the sheep-skin collar of her tweed coat around her ears, looking around at the gleaming world.

To close the door I've had to lift it onto its one hinge. But the base has caught on a ruck in the mat and jammed. I push the door open again, bend down and tug the sodden web clear.

Something metallic has rolled from under the mat onto the threshold slate. I manage this time to close the door. Then I bend down and pick up – I pick up my wedding ring.

Fiona calls: "What have you got there?"

I'm studying the ring. Someone has engraved in the platinum what looks like a child's head. Know what – it's the centre part of the triptych, the one Corny gave me in the dream.

I walk over to show Fiona. "There," I say, "back to normality."

As I put the ring in her hand there's from somewhere close by an odd screech. Or wail. Or shriek.

"Christ!" I say, "what was that?"

Fiona whispers: "It came from over there, from behind the cottage. Come on."

I follow her, tiptoeing along the east of the cottage in the damp shade. Fiona stops at the corner and peeps round. After a moment she reaches back, grabs my sleeve and silently draws me level with her.

In the jewel-glinting frosty sunlight, on the patch of grass beside the apple-tree, is this cream-white peacock – with the unfurled arch and the umpteen emerald and sapphire eyes of its tail in dazzling display.

A moment or two and it seems to sense we're there. It turns once around as if for our benefit, and then there's a dry clatter of quills as its tail collapses – a rustling train which it hauls after it quickly through a hole in the hedge.

144

Annabel's shouting up the stairs: "Mum says you're to come and carve the goose!"

I'm in the bathroom. I went there for something else but caught sight of myself in the mirror and somehow became involved with looking – looking at me, this familiar, dare I say, self, and back into and through what seems many twilit, smokey mirrors at that other distant self that day in windy September I harvested the onions.

I shout: "Just coming."

Beside the bog, on the stool with the magazines, there's the Christmas edition of *Homespun*. I think: So she celebrated getting shot of Rex by renewing her subscription, good girl.

I'm not intending to be long but I can't resist a flick through the pages. Strong-looking articles on *Milk Sheep*. Also on *Earth Dwellings*. Also, *The Cult of the Black Virgin*

I hear the telephone. It'll be Caruso, I know it. On the run.

Annabel calls from the foot of the stairs.

"Dad, phone. It's a Mr Careswell."

"You mean Caruso."

"No Careswell. Mr Careswell. Do hurry."

"Where's he ringing from?"

"From the health clinic, Besseldon Manor."

"Oh," I say. "Ask him what he wants."

She goes back on the blower, and then, "He says to tell you you can celebrate. It's a success. The punters are all delighted with the conservatory, particularly the gold. He says he's got a Christmas bonus for you!"

"A what!"

"A bonus."

"A Buddha?"

"No dad, a bonus."

"Tell him I'm coming," I shout. "No, tell him it's Christmas. Tell him I hope his plumbing's in order. No, tell him I'll... tell him he may expect a call in the New Year from our new Managing Director."

I'm thinking: Another weird coincidence.

Sometime later I return to the magazine. The classified ads section has grown – it now fills six pages. Rebirthing in Ireland. Why not, if that's what you're into? Matrifocal Massage. The Tarot's Role in Wild Flower Selection.

I sigh. It's probably a sigh of content.

And then I sit up straight. There, right at the end, as if squeezed in at the moment of going to press, just the one cramped little line:

GOLDMAKING. C & SM. Bishopseaton 430.

AUTHOR'S NOTE

Barbara Bapty, to whose memory this story is dedicated, was a maverick (I think she would have chuckled her approval of the original meaning of the word, 'an unbranded beast') – a qualified but independent psychotherapist, perhaps more accurately described as a wise woman, or woman of power. As a child she was brought up virtually wild in the Australian outback, and the resulting untamed, free-spirited quality never left her. She and her husband practised as doctors in rural Central Africa, and together brought up a large family. And then in mid-life she discovered and from then on devoted herself to her gift for psychotherapy.

Whatever training she accepted she merely adapted to her own fiercely protected intuitive approach. She simply would not question that the individual psyche, when given the secure opportunity to free itself of the formative 'scarring' of convention and trauma, would of itself and by natural process achieve integration and healing. As she saw it, the source of any 'psyche problem' lay unresolved in feeling – the pain response to past experience that consciousness had been unwilling to live with and so repressed in the unconscious, only for its effect to continue.

Until fully acknowledged, and so integrated with consciousness, the consequences of this 'occluded life' would persist, and might range from trivial mood-swing and depression to serious psychosomatic illness and even, as Barbara would prove, instances of mislabelled schizophrenia. Her way was by some attribute of her power to enable whomever she was accompanying to allow those long-repressed feelings to register and express themselves.

That expression, most often amplified over time by repressed anger, resentment or whatever, and often mythologised in the medium of dream or nightmare, could be dramatic, disturbing, perhaps even terrifying – were it not that Barbara was totally unfazed by anything these feelings could throw up. Her presence was itself reassurance, and she would without intruding preside with inexhaustible compassion and, it must be said, mischievous delight. It was Barbara who convinced me that the capacity for healing, certainly when related to the psyche, is limited or unlimited by the degree of fearlessness of the healer him or herself. Barbara Bapty was fearless.

I myself worked with Barbara in a series of maybe half a dozen sessions. So I need strenuously to distance myself from the experience of the, lets give him the title, hero, as well as every detail of his story (believe it if you will!). Just as of course, I should stress that while Barbara might have had some influence on SM, there was nothing in their appearance, behaviour or language they had in common.

One thing I would say is that as a result of my own experience I find nothing that happens to the hero: the synchronicities, the seemingly paranormal, altogether improbable or, at a time when 'unconscious ingredients' are suddenly volatile, out of place. And if any reader should find unlikely the involvement of the Alchemical, and the detailed way it informs the incidents and the dreams, then perhaps they themselves are ready for a dose of C.G.Jung's masterpiece, *Psychology & Alchemy*.

John Moat
Welcombe, Devon
March 2011